Praise for *Know Your Enemy* and *Beware Your Enemy*

'Comparisons with John Grisham and Vince Flynn are inevitable, but are they justified? Absolutely! There is no better test of a novel than whether you are able to put it down. *Know Your Enemy* passed that test with flying colours. This is a compelling piece of fiction, and to those of you in professional partnerships, you will appreciate more than most the intrigues of the character structures, the loyalties, personalities, greediness and sheer skullduggery of those that sit around that large table. Rod has written this novel in short, fast-paced chapters – relatable characters, easy to read and full of suspense to the very end.'

Michael Hawkins, AM FAICD

'Fast-moving thriller that takes the reader at lightning pace through the ruthless world of illegal financing and boardroom chicanery. Rod Besley's background provides readers with an informed ringside seat to this dynamic, jolting tale set in a world of "whatever it takes". The characters come to life as you experience the gripping tension and right-hand turns through to the thrilling end.'

Greg Meek, former CEO

'*Know Your Enemy* is a fast-moving and suspenseful legal thriller. Tom Jackson uncovers with surgical precision the murky side of property development, international finance, gambling, corruption and money laundering – and how they can and do interact in the 21st-century global economy.... I expect more Tom Jackson thrillers to follow and, in due course, movie rights and movies to challenge the high watermark of John Grisham's *The Firm*.'

Scott McDonald, Law Firm Partner

'Rod Besley has delivered another outstanding story with *Beware Your Enemy*. This fast-paced, compelling read delves into the immense sums generated by modern criminal activities and their laundering through big business. The intrigue and dangers portrayed make this book incredibly hard to put down! Rod's novels stand shoulder to shoulder with bestselling legal thriller authors like John Grisham and Peter Temple, but with a unique twist that extends beyond courtroom dramas. Leveraging his legal expertise, Rod provides readers with an insider's view into the murky and ruthless world of high finance.' **Leighton Trafford, Reviewer**

'Tom Jackson is fast developing into a cult hero; a hybrid of James Bond and a John Grisham protagonist. He requires all of the skills that this combination brings to him to navigate through the intrigue, danger and excitement that is *Beware Your Enemy*. Highly enjoyable.' **Stephen Quartermain, Lawyer**

'In this second novel in the Tom Jackson series, Rod Besley has been able to continue the fast-moving action as Jackson reunites with characters from the first novel, unravelling the twists and turns of another high-profile international property deal linked with funding from suspect sources. From central London to Cairo the action never ceases from start to finish. Another unputdownable read that will have you turning the pages well into the night.'

Peter O'Donnell

'Tour de force in the legal thriller genre. *Know Your Enemy* is more than just a legal thriller; it's an addictive reading experience. Besley's debut is a resounding success, captivating readers with its intellectual rigor and breakneck pacing. This book is an absolute must-read, guaranteeing an enthralling journey through the complex webs of legal intrigue and power. Once you start reading, you simply can't put it down – a testament to Besley's prowess as a storyteller in this riveting legal drama.'

Hugh, United States Verified Reviewer

A Tom Jackson Legal Thriller

ROD BESLEY

Vanquish Your Enemy

Cover designed by Judith San Nicolas
Printed and bound in Australia by IngramSpark
Prepared for publication and edited by Dr Juliette Lachemeier at The Erudite Pen
(theeruditepen.com)

 A catalogue record for this
book is available from the
National Library of Australia

Vanquish Your Enemy: A Tom Jackson Legal Thriller (Book 3)
ISBN 9780645902747
E-ISBN 9780645902754

I dedicate this book, and every book I write, to you, Karen, my partner in life and soulmate. Your unconditional love and endless patience are the source of my strength. I cherish every one of the fifty years we have been together. May there be many more.

Your husband, Rod.

Prologue

Monday, October 1, 2017

'Now what do we do with him?' she said with a twisted grin on her face, part fascination, part concern, looking down at the prone figure of Jason Jones.

Murray Jensen looked up at Luna Smythe while checking Jones' pulse to make sure he hadn't held the choke hold on him for too long. Satisfied that he hadn't, Jensen injected the drug from the syringe he'd carried in his pocket, after carefully removing the cap.

'He'll sleep like a baby for several hours after what I've just given him. He's a big bastard so I gave him an extra-large dose, just to make sure.'

Jensen was also a large man, having honed his physique over the years with a near obsessive commitment to exercise workouts. In his early fifties, Jensen was unhappy most of the time, except when immersed in an operation on behalf of one of his many ruthless criminal clients somewhere in the world.

As he stood over the helpless figure at his feet, his mouth formed a genuine smile. His obsidian-like eyes, however, conveyed a different emotion. He wanted revenge. Jason Jones and Australian-based lawyer, Tom Jackson, had inflicted significant, although not fatal, damage to the London-based operation of his global killer-for-hire business.

'We take him with us to South America. On the way, I'll figure out how best to use the capture of Jones as leverage against Tom Jackson.'

'Have you thought this through? Won't he hamper our efforts to disappear?' Luna Smythe grimaced as she asked what seemed obvious questions.

Jensen silenced her with a steely gaze, then pointed to the wheelchair he had directed Smythe to bring with her to the Royal Botanic Gardens in Sydney, in anticipation of successfully apprehending Jones. He knew that most of those who worked for him were fearful of his near-psychopathic persona, and he could see from the instant fear in Luna's eyes that she was no exception. Still fuming at her gall to question his motives, he silently questioned himself. She had made a valid point, but for now he would stay the course and secure Jones, until he developed a plan to exact revenge on Tom Jackson.

In the shadow of the faulty light, Jensen and Smythe lifted Jason Jones into the wheelchair and headed for their nearby parked vehicle.

Their nearly two-hour road trip to the secluded airstrip in the New South Wales Southern Highlands was uneventful. Jensen had called ahead to their pilot, who had the private jet on standby. The plan was to fly to a private airstrip in the North Island of New Zealand to refuel, before heading to South America.

With the assistance of the pilot, they loaded the still unconscious Jason Jones on to the plane, checked his restraints and secured his seatbelt.

Once they had taken their comfortable seats on the private jet and fastened their own seatbelts, Murray Jensen turned his head to look across the aisle at Luna Smythe.

'I know you rescued me from incarceration, Luna, and I'm grateful for that, but never question me again.' Jensen's curled upper lip exacerbated the anger evident from his furious face.

Luna's emerald green eyes widened involuntarily, no doubt reflecting again on her poor judgement in confronting Jensen. Luna was a single, attractive woman in her mid-thirties. She had not had any success with relationships, and not for want of trying. Having escaped her own low-security custody following the raids by authorities in London, Luna had hatched an elaborate and daring plan to free Jensen on his way to a maximum-security facility. In so doing, she had permanently hitched her wagon to Jensen's cause, whatever that might be.

'I understand.' Smythe licked her dry lips and lowered her head in submission. She was a technology expert who, until recently, had not been engaged in any kind of field operations.

Jensen simply grunted and looked out the window as the private jet sped down the grass runway, headed for New Zealand.

Once the jet had reached cruising altitude, Jensen resumed a less aggressive manner towards Luna. Apart from his gratitude for his surprise release from the authorities, he would need her technical expertise to assist with the rebuilding of his operations from another location.

'We have a lot to do, Luna, to get things back on track. I agree that we should not let Jones interrupt that process, and if I can't think of a sensible and expeditious way to use Jones against Tom Jackson, we'll just dispense with him and move on. We're headed to another private airstrip in New Zealand's North Island, located on a farm not far from New Plymouth. We'll refuel there and head for Ecuador in South America. Jones will likely be awake by the time we land in New Zealand, and I will by then have worked out what to do with him. A quick termination is shaping up as the most likely outcome, perhaps via live video feed to his annoying buddy, Tom Jackson.'

*

Jones was already awake and listening intently to their sinister plan. He was, indeed, a large man. In his mid-forties, and a little under 6 foot tall, Jones was a special forces veteran, having served three tours of Afghanistan. He worked out on an almost daily basis, and was highly trained in the martial art of Krav Maga, the official martial art of the Israeli Defence Force and its Elite Units.

He resolved to feign his unconscious state for as long as possible, in an effort to gain as much knowledge about Jensen's plans as he could. Having heard the plan to terminate him upon landing in New Zealand, he knew he had to escape at the first available opportunity.

Jones was 'shaken awake' by Murray Jensen sometime later, after a bumpy landing on the private airstrip. He looked out the window and was momentarily taken aback by the sheer beauty of his surroundings. The airstrip was high on a ridge, overlooking lush rolling green hills peppered with numerous herds of sheep and black cattle he knew to be Angus beef cattle. Not too far away he could see the majestic snow-capped Mount Taranaki rising above the surrounding farmlands.

Refocusing his attention, Jones allowed himself to be roughly removed from the plane. He pretended to be groggy and generally unsteady on his feet, knowing this would allow his captors to treat him as a lesser threat, for now.

Murray Jensen took out a satellite phone and dialled Tom Jackson's number in Brisbane, Australia. Jensen was distracted as he heard Tom's voice and began with delight to tell him he'd captured his colleague Jason Jones, and that Jackson was about to witness his execution.

Now or never, Jones said to himself. He charged at Murray Jensen, knocking him over. Jensen let go of the satellite phone while in flight, and hit the ground hard. Jones wasted no time in landing several strategic kicks to Jensen. He managed to bring his tied hands to the front of his body by looping them under his feet, and he followed up the kicks to Jensen with a savage double-handed blow to the side of his head.

Thinking quickly, Jones grabbed Jensen's gun from his belt and pointed it at the pilot and Luna Smythe, who had both watched in horror as the events unfolded with lightning speed.

'Grab a knife and cut me loose,' he commanded. Smythe obliged, as quickly as she could. 'Now use the spare cable ties I am sure you must have on board to tie Jensen, and no unexpected moves from either of you, or you won't be long for this world.'

Still suffering from the effects of the drug that Jensen had administered, Jones ran through all the options in his head. He knew he wasn't thinking clearly. He should probably restrain all of them and contact the authorities. *Where was that phone?* Momentarily distracted with his groggy thought process, Jones failed to notice the pilot reaching behind his back. It was a split-second lapse, and now he was looking into the barrel of a small gun in the pilot's outstretched hand.

'I wouldn't if I were you,' Jones growled.

The pilot held his nerve, although his hand was shaking. 'It's a small gun, but I can't miss you at this distance.'

Jones could see that the pilot wasn't bluffing. *Mexican standoff. Fuck!* He backed away slowly until he was out of accuracy range of the pilot's gun, before turning to run off unsteadily down the hillside and head for the nearest farmhouse to raise the alarm.

Luna Smythe and the pilot were left staring at the receding figure of Jones. They looked at the unconscious Jensen and nodded to each other. Without a word between them, they hoisted Murray Jensen aboard the plane, checked that the refuelling was complete, and made preparations to depart.

Chapter 1

Six months later (April 2, 2018)

DAY 1 (Monday)

Tom Jackson sat at his desk, looking out the window from level 30 of his Mary Street office in central Brisbane. Jackson was a partner in the Brisbane office of Ridgeway Mason, a successful Australian law firm.

Tom was again reflecting on recent events, and in particular the escape by his good friend Jason Jones from the clutches of ruthless criminal Murray Jensen six months earlier. He thought he had heard the last of Jensen after he and Jones, with the assistance of Australian and UK INTERPOL, had successfully dismantled Jensen's London operations. Against all odds, Jensen had escaped on his way to a maximum-security facility. He knew Jensen was resourceful, but no one had expected to hear from him so soon after the events in London had unfolded.

When Murray Jensen called Tom from New Zealand to boast that he had captured Jason, and was about to execute him on a live video feed to Tom, his blood ran cold. One minute he was speaking with Jensen, and the next the satellite phone had gone dead. Thinking the worst, he had immediately contacted Inspector

Lachlan Darwin at his Australian INTERPOL headquarters in Canberra.

Tom was relieved to receive a call from Jason Jones not long after he had made contact with Inspector Darwin, confirming that he had immobilised Murray Jensen, but had failed to capture him after the pilot had produced a gun while Jason was groggy and distracted. Jones had been annoyed with his lapse of concentration and had resolved that escape to a nearby farmhouse was his best option. He said he'd seen the private jet take off soon after he'd escaped.

Both now in their mid-forties, Tom Jackson and Jason Jones met when Tom was studying law at university nearly twenty years ago. Jones had completed his business and finance studies by then, and they met when Tom started training in the Krav Maga martial art. Their training had served them both well over the last couple of years in particular, having to deal with unexpected physical encounters with extremely dangerous criminal lowlifes.

He dialled Jason Jones' number.

'Hey, Tom. How the hell are ya, mate. I've been thinking of you a bit lately.'

'Likewise, Jason. I've just been reflecting on the events in New Zealand and what led to them. Heard anything from Inspector Darwin yet?'

'Nada, mate. You?'

'Like you, nothing at all.'

After Jason returned to Australia, they had linked up with Inspector Darwin. Jones had relayed all of the information he'd heard on the plane while feigning unconsciousness. So far, Darwin had been unable to trace the whereabouts of Jensen's private jet, and aggressive questioning of the owners of the private airstrip in New Zealand had not revealed anything. Murray Jensen was too experienced to leave any kind of trail, and the airstrip owners had gratefully accepted the huge cash payment for the use of the airstrip, without question.

'It's been six months,' Tom continued hopefully, a slight smile creeping across his face. 'Maybe that's the last we'll hear of him.'

'I hope you're right, mate. Unfortunately, I think he's a vengeful bastard who will likely have a long memory. I know the trail has gone cold, but we should not let our guard down. We need to also remember that two members of the Hong Kong-based criminal syndicate we brought down managed to escape, and I expect they too will be quietly rebuilding their operation. Not sure if they'll ever reconnect with Murray Jensen.'

'Anything's possible, I guess.' Tom looked at the buildings in the distance, deep in thought. 'I think it's unlikely, although I agree we should not let our guard down. They are ruthless enemies who I expect will stop at nothing to exact revenge if the opportunity presented itself.

'Anyway, Jason, just thought I'd check in with you. I need to refocus on my latest transaction. My Australian-based theme park owner has engaged me to assist with the sale of a theme park they own in Italy, just outside Rome.'

'Sounds like a cracker deal, mate. Enjoy!'

'Thanks, Jase. Stay out of trouble and chat soon.'

'Roger that.'

Tom Jackson returned his attention to his computer to revisit the latest email correspondence on the €200 million theme park deal. His Australian-based client owned one of the theme parks between Brisbane and the Gold Coast. Their operations had been extremely successful, allowing them to purchase several theme parks around the world. After each purchase, they injected large amounts of capital to expand the operations of the park to include the latest rides and attractions. This was the first time they had decided to divest a revamped asset. It was interesting work. Tom undertook as much of the legal work as he could, and engaged lawyers in the country in question where necessary and appropriate. On this occasion, he was planning to work with the Italian office of global law firm Andrich Wiley. A London-based colleague had recommended Lorenzo Bassutri in the Rome office of Andrich Wiley.

Tom had not yet made contact with Bassutri, nor had he been provided with complete details of the buyer. All he knew was that the buyer entity had recently been incorporated in London, and that they would be arranging finance at the same time as negotiating the Terms Sheet and acquisition agreements. Thankfully the documents were in English. Jackson had dealt with foreign language contracts in the past, and was glad on this occasion to avoid the added layer of complexity that entailed.

He was in the process of reviewing the latest version of the Terms Sheet, and his plan was to revert to his client sometime tomorrow with his preliminary comments and suggested amendments.

For now, it was time to head home to his inner western suburbs home in Brisbane for a regular evening workout in his well-equipped home gym.

Chapter 2

Initially, Murray Jensen was furious. Jason Jones had bested him on the private airstrip in New Zealand six months ago, and escaped. Instead of freeing Jensen, allowing him to recover and then pursue and recapture Jones, Luna Smythe, aided by the pilot of his private jet, had carried him on to the plane in an unconscious state. The plane had departed immediately, headed for their next refuelling stop on the way to Ecuador.

Common sense had, however, prevailed, and by the time they reached their next refuelling stopover, his logical dispassionate thinking had taken control. Smythe had been right all along. What had he been thinking when he decided to bring the captured Jason Jones with him? He should have just killed him and dumped the body in a remote area on the way to their jet in the New South Wales Southern Highlands. He could then have dealt with Tom Jackson at a later date. Now he still had to contend with both of them! Better to do so from a position of strength.

Murray Jensen had worked hard over the last few decades to establish his global business providing services to his well-resourced criminal clients. He was fortunate enough to be able to choose his clients now, and he only accepted work from what he regarded as apex criminal organisations. His services ranged from surveillance and intimidation through to assassinations. Some assassinations were subtle and made to look like accidents. Others were outright brutal and designed to send a clear message to someone. He had developed these skills himself at an early age, as a means of survival while growing up on the streets of London. He was a natural leader and quickly realised that by marshalling those loyal to him, he could service the voracious appetites of criminals who required others to do their dirty work. It constantly surprised him just how much people were prepared to pay for his services. It enabled him to employ and train only the best operatives. Over the years, his business had successfully expanded into a global network.

Up until the events that had unfolded in London last year, his reputation had been beyond reproach. Thanks to Tom Jackson and Jason Jones, that was no longer the case. He would get even with those two fuckers if it was the last thing he did.

His plan in initially heading to Ecuador had a twofold purpose. First, it would allow him to escape the authorities. He was confident they would not be able to trace his whereabouts. Second, it would allow him to re-establish both his global network and his reputation. Luna Smythe would be invaluable with the technical logistics of reconnecting his network. There was no better way in his mind to rebuild his reputation than to personally undertake wetwork for the powerful Colombian drug cartels. In the past, he had always had an overseer role in this type of work for clients.

Six months ago, they had flown direct to Coca, 300 kilometres due east of Quito, the capital of Ecuador. From there they had travelled for two hours by speed boat with the current of the Napo River, a tributary to the Amazon River that rises in Ecuador on the flanks of the east Andean volcanoes. Jensen was momentarily transported back to the boat ride. The volume and rate of flow of the water had been something to behold. As was the lush jungle and abundant wildlife that crowded the edges of the fast-flowing river. He recalled seeing all kinds of vibrantly coloured birds and hearing the constant chatter of monkeys as they darted from tree to tree. It was a far cry from the concrete jungle of London.

They had arrived at a remote camp which, from the river, looked like any other rudimentary mining camp in the area. Once inside the settlement, however, which was mostly protected from aerial surveillance by camouflage netting, he had realised just how sophisticated the small village was. It was carved out of the dense Amazon jungle with very little unused cleared areas, in an effort to avoid detection from the air. Jensen had seen several workers who seemed to be tasked with keeping the fast-growing jungle at bay.

A helicopter landing pad was located within the village. It was occupied by a Comanche advanced armed reconnaissance and attack helicopter. By arrangement, the head of security for one of the largest South American drug cartels had travelled to the settlement to meet with Jensen. He had provided Jensen with a wide-ranging brief to eliminate the upper echelons of a rival cartel that had apparently transgressed the terms of an unwritten law between the cartels.

Within a relatively short space of time, Jensen had assembled the required resources and clinically implemented the brief, dispatching everyone on the list he had been provided with. The assassinations took place, without recourse, across many countries throughout South and Central America. It felt good to be involved at the coalface again, and it had given him first-hand knowledge of the skillsets of his pre-existing and new recruits.

He was ready to return to the global stage, and had convinced the Colombian drug cartel that he could facilitate some of their money laundering needs. Impressed with what he had achieved for them within a relatively short timeframe, they agreed to allow him to explore the possibility.

Murray Jensen reached out to the two members of the Hong Kong-based syndicate who'd managed to escape the wide net that had been cast over their operations. Money laundering was their specialty.

'We need to meet soon, Yu and Xiao,' Jensen said to Yen Chow Yu and Ping Xiaoyan, both of whom were on the pre-arranged and secure conference call.

Yen Chow Yu and Ping Xiaoyan had fled Hong Kong after the capture of the other seven members of their criminal syndicate six months ago. They'd reconnected with each other three months later in southern Portugal and successfully resumed their criminal activities. Most of the cash the syndicate had squirrelled away was tied up in numbered Swiss bank accounts they were loath to access just yet. They were in the process of rebuilding capital reserves from their remaining illicit gambling businesses and depositing the funds to newly created Swiss bank accounts. Jensen's call had been timely. It would not be long before they were again looking to resume the other key activity of their business: money laundering.

Jensen's offer to engage them to assist with laundering drug cartel monies represented an opportunity to accelerate their plans. While they did not usually undertake such work for third parties, they were not willing to pass up the chance to resume lucrative money laundering activities sooner than they had expected.

Chapter 3

'Ciao.' Lorenzo Bassutri answered his mobile phone after it nearly rang out, with typical Italian flair.

Rome was eight hours behind Brisbane, and Tom had left it until six p.m. Brisbane time – ten a.m. in Rome – just to make sure Lorenzo would be in the office. Italian lawyers were not known to be early starters, although they usually worked late.

Jackson loved Italy and everything about it. The people, the food and the language. Whenever Tom visited Italy, everything seemed so much more laid back and simple. The Italian language itself was the most obvious manifestation of this, and was regarded as one of the world's most beautiful languages. The Italian alphabet, derived from the Latin one, contained only twenty-one letters. Grammatical constructs and pronunciations had evolved to intentionally make the language more pleasant.

'Buongiorno, Lorenzo.' Tom chose the slightly more formal salutation, notwithstanding Lorenzo's informality. 'My name is Tom Jackson, and I am a transaction lawyer based in Brisbane, Australia. While we haven't been formally introduced, a colleague of mine in London has recommended I seek your assistance with the legal aspects of a deal I'm working on in Italy for an Australian client.'

'Ah, si, Signor Jackson.'

'Tom, please Lorenzo.'

'Si, Tom. Elwood Watson from Brentworth Watson Doyle in London has already been in contact, and mentioned you would be calling soon. I have dealt with Signor Elwood on many occasions. He has briefly mentioned to me the dealings the two of you had last year in London, and not unlike many other lawyers in our sphere of expertise, I am in awe. You must tell me more about it someday, Tom. I am, of course, also well aware of your globally recognised professional reputation.'

'Perhaps one day, Lorenzo, while we sip a limoncello overlooking the sights of Rome. For now, however, I'd like to enlist your assistance on an imminent deal for the sale of the Mondo Dei Sogni theme park just outside Rome.' Tom did not wish to dwell on the events of last year in London and Cairo. Aspects of what transpired were personally very traumatic, and a lot of people had lost their lives. Tom had almost lost his own life, having been shot in the head by one of his captors while trying to escape. Fortunately, the bullet had only grazed the side of his head.

'Inteso, understood, Tom. Scusa, sorry. I will look forward to our discussions on this. Limoncello is my favourite drink after an evening meal, and it might aid in the digestion of what I understand to be an enthralling story.

'I am very familiar with Mondo Dei Sogni, the Italian 'Dreamworld' theme park just outside Rome. I have two children of my own and we are season pass holders.'

'No need to apologise, Lorenzo. I had hoped you'd have knowledge of the theme park. I always find it useful to understand the physical attributes of an asset, as well as its legal nuances. It's only very early days in the deal, and document negotiation has just commenced. I'm aware a deal of this nature fits squarely within your expertise and was hoping you would have sufficient capacity to assist me.'

'Assolutamente, absolutely. I would be delighted to assist you with the deal, grazie mille, Tom. I have a large team at my disposal in Andrich Wiley, and can easily shuffle things around to free up some personal capacity. Can you send me some information on the deal, please, and we can settle on a formal retainer arrangement.'

'I'm glad you're able to assist, thanks Lorenzo. I'll send some information this evening. If you respond during your working day, I'll get back to you tomorrow my time.'

'Will you be travelling to Rome, Tom?'

'Assolutamente, absolutely.' Tom grinned inwardly. 'Italy is my favourite country in the world to visit. In a professional sense, I find it's always best to be on site with deals of this nature. Apart from anything else, we will then be in the same time zone, which will make things much easier. The lawyers for the proposed buyer are in London. I'll need to sort out my own workflow and logistics, and of course deal with the usual law firm internal politics.'

'Fantastico, Tom. I understand completely the internal law firm issues you will need to deal with. I am sure it is the same the world over. The 'what's in it for me' attitude is a dominant force in professional firms.' Lorenzo chuckled loudly.

Tom already liked Lorenzo Bassutri and was looking forward to working with him. Expertise and reputation could be easily researched, and he had already verified Lorenzo's credentials not long after he had been referred to him. There were many good lawyers, however, who were unnecessarily challenging to deal with. Lorenzo did not seem to suffer from that shortcoming.

Tom had pre-prepared a brief for Lorenzo, in anticipation of his being available to assist. He emailed the brief to Lorenzo immediately after their call ended. There weren't many lawyers who would pass up the opportunity to be involved in a complex €200 million sale transaction.

Tom's next call was to long-time colleague Max Grenfell, also a senior partner in the Brisbane office of Ridgeway Mason. Max and Tom knew each other at university, and had reconnected at Ridgeway Mason not long after Tom finished his degree. Max was a few years older than Tom and had spent the intervening years at a boutique law firm in central London.

'Hey, Max. Not too late I hope?'

'Not at all, Tom. Happy to chat with you anytime. We've both been so busy lately we haven't had much of a chance to connect. How're things progressing with the Italian theme park deal you mentioned briefly at the last partners' meeting?'

'Good instincts as usual, as that's exactly what I'm calling you about. I'm just about to engage a partner in the Rome office of global law firm Andrich Wiley. A fellow by the name of Lorenzo Bassutri, who comes highly recommended by Ellwood Watson in London. I'm planning to travel to Rome and remain there for the duration of the transaction. As with most of the deals my clients bring to me, this one has a very tight time frame. It'll be much easier to be in the same time zone as Lorenzo, and also the buyer's lawyers who are based in London. I should be able to supervise most of my other work remotely, although it would be very helpful if you could again please assist with local supervision. I'd feel a little vulnerable heading overseas for any length of time without someone like you looking after my team and my interests in general in the Brisbane office.'

'Not a problem, mate. I've got your back. I expect you'll be heading to Italy well before the next scheduled partners' meeting? I suggest you have a chat to Fred, and then send an email to our fellow business proprietors. Fred's a good bloke, and will smooth over any ruffled feathers at the next meeting. I'll make sure I'm also there to support you.'

Tom could almost see Max wrinkling his nose at the thought of the attitudes of some of their partners. For some reason, which continued to perplex both Max and Tom, not all of their fellow business proprietors were supportive of each other's success. Perhaps it was just an outward display of their insecurity. Petty jealousies were rife in law firms, and in particular the larger ones. Tom and Max had learnt long ago that unconditional professional support from someone within the same environment was both essential and rare.

Frederick Anderson was the Brisbane office's managing partner. He was a good leader, who had a lot of respect for Jackson. The feeling was mutual.

'That was my thinking as well. I'll go and see Fred tomorrow. Thanks for the chat, Max. Enjoy your evening.'

Chapter 4

DAY 2 (Tuesday)

Tom Jackson arrived at the office early. He was usually first in and last to leave. Not out of any misconceived desire to be heroic by wearing the 'I'm the busiest' badge of honour, but rather from necessity. His many clients demanded exceptionally high standards from him, and he had fostered those expectations by consistently delivering on the brief. While he had a great team of lawyers at his disposal, whose contributions were invaluable, his clients all insisted that he have final sign-off on all key aspects of the work. Many would prefer him to simply clone himself, if that were possible. Some had even said as much.

Jackson had sent an email message overnight to the Brisbane office's managing partner, Frederick Anderson, requesting a brief meeting first thing, assuming he was available. As he was reflecting with delight on his forthcoming trip to Italy, Tom's phone rang.

'Morning, Tom. Does now work for you?'

'Sure, Fred. See you shortly.'

Frederick Anderson's office was in the north-eastern corner on level 30, not far from Tom's office. Anderson was a cycling fanatic and usually arrived early after cycling to the office from the outer western suburbs of Brisbane. Although the distance from his acreage to the office was roughly twenty kilometres, Anderson always took one of many alternative circuitous routes to ensure he cycled at least thirty kilometres. His tall, athletic physique amplified his presence as a leader, and was the envy of many others who were also in their late fifties.

'Grab a seat, Tom.' Anderson's full head of stylishly trimmed grey hair was still damp from his early morning post-cycle shower in the basement facilities.

'You mentioned in your email that you wanted to discuss the Italian theme park sale deal. Has it progressed?'

'It sure has. I've received the first revision of the Terms Sheet from the proposed buyer's London lawyers. I've also done some preliminary drafting of the primary acquisition documents, and it won't be long before we are well underway with document negotiations. I've reached out to Lorenzo Bassutri in the Rome office of Andrich Wiley, and he has responded overnight with a very reasonable retainer arrangement. I've sent this to my client together with a favourable recommendation. Lorenzo is highly recommended by Ellwood Watson from London-based firm Brentworth Watson Doyle.'

'I've not heard of Lorenzo, but have had many dealings with other partners from Andrich Wiley in various countries. Great firm. Watson's personal recommendation should also give you a high level of comfort.'

'I know how you work, Tom, so I suppose you're here to tell me you'll be heading to Rome shortly.'

'Tomorrow, in fact, Fred. I've had a chat to Max Grenfell and he's agreed to again provide oversight to my team and their work while I am away. With your consent I propose to send a brief email to all Brisbane partners to let them know I'll be based in Italy for the duration of the transaction. I briefly raised the prospect of this at the last partners' meeting, so there shouldn't be any issues.'

'Granted,' Anderson said in an over-exaggerated manner.

Tom looked up from his notes to see Anderson grinning broadly. They hadn't always seen eye to eye. Events over the last year had cemented their relationship into one based on significant mutual trust. Tom's initial surprised look was quickly replaced with a matching grin.

'I'll cover off on any issues in the next partners' meeting, and I'm sure Max will be there to assist if need be. Let me know if there's anything else you need me to do for you.'

'Will do, and thanks. I'll keep you in the loop by email on key developments in the deal.'

As he headed back to his office, Tom allowed his thoughts to wander. He loved Italy, and Rome in particular. Not for the first time he found himself feeling grateful for the extraordinary opportunities his chosen profession offered to him. He was certain things would be busy in Rome, but knew he would have some time to soak up the culture and history of the magnificent city. He was enamoured of all that Rome had to offer, not the least of which were the Colosseum, the Roman Forum, and one of his favourite locations, Piazza Navona. Authorities were still uncovering historical sites and artefacts from there on an almost daily basis.

Thinking of Rome made him think of his estranged wife, Mary Jackson. The last time he had been in Rome was with Mary. They had separated more than two years ago, and it had become apparent that there was no prospect of a reconciliation. Mary was a successful forensic accountant in a Brisbane firm. He was aware that she had been in a relationship for around six months. He made a mental note to speak with Mary about formalising a divorce after he returned from Rome.

Even though separated, each maintained a healthy respect for the other, and was genuinely concerned for their wellbeing. They shared a mutual understanding that each would tell the other of any planned overseas travel. Events of the last two years had reminded them that life was short, and could come to an abrupt halt at any time. Tom's inadvertent interactions with criminal elements during that period had afforded many unpleasant examples of that.

'Mary, got a minute.' Mary Jackson usually answered her mobile phone when Tom rang, even if she was in a meeting.

'Sure, Tom. Let me step out of this meeting.' Once outside the meeting room, Mary continued, concern immediately evident in her voice. 'Is everything okay? You don't usually call during work hours.'

'Yes, and sorry. I was just thinking about you and thought I'd give you a quick call to let you know I'm headed to Rome for a few weeks to work on a theme park deal over there.'

'That's nice for you. I remember our last trip to Italy together. We both love that country.'

Tom could visualise her blue-green eyes, and the dreamy nostalgic look on her face. 'I'm leaving tomorrow and should be back before the end of the month. If there is any reason why you can't contact me by email or mobile, Max will know how to get in touch.'

'Okay, Tom. Thanks for letting me know. I'd better get back to my meeting.' And then, almost as if it were an afterthought, 'Have you spoken with Jason Jones, just to put him in the picture?'

'I hadn't planned on doing that, but you're right, of course. I'll give him a call shortly. Can't be too careful after the events of the last couple of years.'

'Exactly, and Tom…'

'Yes?'

'Take care of yourself.'

With Mary's words ringing in his ears, he rose from his desk to close the door to his office, and dialled Jason Jones' number.

'Tom, what the fuck, mate? I don't hear from you for friggin' ages, and then twice in two days. Everything okay?'

Tom couldn't help but smile at Jason's typical profanity, which served to lighten his mood a little. 'As far as I'm aware, yes. I've just been chatting with Mary and she thought it best that I let you know the details of my trip to Rome tomorrow, just in case. I have no reason to think there is anything untoward about this deal, but I respect her instincts and thought I'd bring you up to speed.'

Tom spent the next ten minutes giving Jones a brief rundown on the logistics of the deal, careful not to disclose any client confidences. He might need Jason's assistance, although he doubted it. That would be the time to sign him up on a retainer and disclose all known pertinent details.

'Got all that, mate. Hopefully for your sake I won't need to be involved in his one. Don't be afraid to holler if you need me, and I'll be there with bells on.'

'Thanks, Jase. I may need you in connection with funding source verification. I'll let you know. Hopefully there'll be none of the shenanigans of the type we were discussing yesterday.'

'Without wanting to put the kibosh on things, Tom, but any large deal for the sale of an asset in a country with low sovereign risk, including Italy, is like a magnet for scumbags and their ill-gotten gains.'

'Point taken. I won't let my guard down and I'll stay in touch.'

'Roger that. Chat soon, mate.'

Jackson spent the rest of the day finalising his comments on the Terms Sheet that he sent to his client, and in arranging logistics for the ongoing work within his team during his absence. But after Jones' comment about the magnet for scumbags, he couldn't shake the uneasy feeling creeping into his subconsciousness.

Chapter 5

DAY 3 (Wednesday)

Murray Jensen was impressed with how quickly Luna Smythe had managed to re-establish normal communications with his global network. While he and his teams were gallivanting around South and Central America, leaving a trail of bloody destruction wherever they went, Luna had managed to accumulate vast amounts of hardware and set up a secure global network for Jensen's operations. She was confident the new systems were more comprehensive, faster and even more secure than the network that had been dismantled by the authorities in London during their raids six months earlier. This not only spoke to Luna's expertise, but also to the resourcefulness of those running the drug cartel's remote operation in the Amazon jungle.

He had thought about leaving Luna behind, but had decided she would be safer with him. There were not many women in the remote settlement, and no other white women. He had left a guard to watch over her while he and others were off on their killing spree. It had turned out to be a good call, with much evident unhappiness that she was not generally available to the mostly male residents of the village. He thought it a waste of resources to leave a trained operative on babysitting duties. Besides, Luna had set things up so well she could access the secure network from anywhere with her administrative privileges, and that might prove invaluable to Jensen while he was on the move.

Jensen's trained operatives had dissipated in accordance with prearranged protocols after their mission was complete. Murray Jensen was not one to dwell on his mistakes of the past. He learnt from them and moved on. That was not to say he was the forgiving type. He would never forget or forgive the damage Tom Jackson and Jason Jones had inflicted on his operations. Revenge may have to wait a little longer, although one never knew what strange twists of fate might lay ahead.

They left early and travelled against the rapid flow of the Napo River, headed for Coca. The return trip took an extra hour longer than the downstream trip, thanks to the massive volume of water the small motor boat had to conquer on the way to its destination. The boat also had to regularly dodge other vessels moving rapidly with the current in the opposite direction, and countless floating tangled masses of jungle vines that had come adrift from the edges of the jungle and joined together.

Once in Coca, Jensen arranged for he and Smythe to fly to Quito, which was located in the Andean mountains at an altitude of 2,850 metres above sea level. The plane was small and the white-knuckled flight took around forty minutes.

Ashen-faced and sweating, Jensen said, 'I swear I saw the wings of that plane flapping up and down,' as they made their way down the flimsy stairs to the tarmac.

Smythe turned to face him with an equally pallid complexion. The surprise that registered on her face was no doubt as a result of witnessing an outward expression of fear from him. Not many had seen Jensen express anything remotely resembling that emotion. He quickly regathered his composure. 'Shitty flight with all the ups and downs, but the scenery over the mountains was brilliant.'

'Agreed.' Smythe turned quickly to resume her trek to the terminal. She would not have wanted Jensen to witness her reaction to his outward display of that basic human emotion: fear.

As their flight was domestic, there were no issues navigating the terminal after collecting their luggage. Jensen knew that there would not be any X-ray machines and was able to keep his Glock handgun with him. They made their way via taxi into central Quito to the five-star Swissôtel Quito in Avenida 12 de Octubre.

Jensen had been to Quito a few years ago and had been fortunate enough to witness the weekly spectacular changing of the guard. It took place every Monday morning at the Plaza Grande in the Old Town of Quito. Jensen explained to Smythe on the way to their hotel that the ceremony had its origins in the early nineteenth century when Ecuador gained independence from Spanish colonialists. The tradition has continued on a weekly basis since then with all the pomp and ceremony, including traditional uniforms. It was a huge tourist attraction, although conspiracy theorists maintained that the President was quite a suspicious person and felt safer to rotate his guards on a weekly basis. As a professional assassin, Jensen could not see the logic in this, but at the time had chosen not to dwell too much on that thought process.

'I've arranged for us to visit a contact this evening to collect our travel documents,' he said.

After settling in to their luxurious hotel, Jensen and Smythe joined the lively throng of tourists and locals in the vibrant streets of downtown Quito. Jensen knew that Quito could be a dangerous place for tourists, particularly in the evenings, and had said as much to Luna. She acknowledged his warning and was happy for him to take the lead. That did not prevent her from enjoying the sights and sounds of the historic city as well as the surrounding mountains, many of which were snow-capped and rose up to 2,000 metres above the city.

Jensen took them to a preselected destination – a small restaurant not far from the busy streets. They were shown to a booth in the rear of the restaurant by its owner, who whispered something into Jensen's ear on the way in, subtly nodding in the direction of the rear section. Luna thought nothing of it and set about interpreting the menu, which was almost entirely in Spanish. Even though her Spanish could at best be described as conversational, interpretation was no trouble to a tech-savvy person. In moments she had sourced an App that translated the menu via the camera on her smart phone. Jensen saw that she was reading the menu in English on the screen of her phone. He was impressed, although he didn't need the assistance as he spoke Spanish.

'Is there anything you don't like or can't eat?' Jensen asked Luna.

'It all looks great. I'm happy for you to order for both of us, thanks.' Smythe seemed happy to defer to Jensen, as she should be. He was, after all, a well-known control freak, even in respect to such relatively mundane matters as ordering food in a restaurant.

Murray Jensen summoned the waiter and then, in fluent Spanish, ordered a selection of tapas-style plates for them to share.

Both devoured the delicious food on the plates as soon as they appeared. Neither had eaten since breakfast. Eating anything on the short plane trip from Coca, or at the airport at either end, had not been an option for either of them.

Immediately after the final plate of food had been devoured, Jensen stood abruptly and headed for the rear of the restaurant, gesturing for Luna to follow him. She did so without question.

They entered a room at the back of the restaurant through a door that was not visible to customers. A small figure turned to them from a desk he was working at in the corner. The lighting was dim except for the lamp on the desk.

'Buenas noches, good evening, Senor and Senora. I have been expecting you. The travel documents are almost ready. All I need is a passport photo of each of you.' The man spoke entirely in Spanish.

'Gracias, thank you.'

The document forger went quietly about his business, and within fifteen minutes he handed them their new travel documents. The passports identified them as a married couple who were Spanish nationals. Maya and Luis Sanchez. In comparison to his last set of travel documents, Murray Jensen was almost unrecognisable, having shaved his trademark dreadlocks prior to travelling to Australia to capture Jones. Smythe had also undergone a transformation while in the remote settlement. She now wore her previously shoulder-length ash blonde hair much shorter and coloured chestnut brown.

Luna looked at the documents handed to her, and then up at Jensen. 'Married, huh. I do hope you won't be expecting anything marital-related?' She had a cheeky grin and a slight twinkle in her emerald green eyes.

Jensen chose to ignore her flippant attitude. 'The authorities won't be looking for a married couple from Spain. The forgers here have connections elsewhere that I have used over the years. They have never let me down. I don't even remotely feel the need to kill this one to ensure he doesn't become a weak link.'

The forger, who until now had pretended he did not understand English, was immediately on alert, his eyes darting to each of the two doors offering an escape route.

Jensen's instincts kicked in. With one hand on the gun in the belt behind his back, he reassured the forger. 'No te preocupes, don't worry, mi amigo.' Jensen reached into his shoulder bag with his other hand and produced a large wad of American dollars.

The forger visibly relaxed, gratefully took the money and began counting. He looked up after he had finished the task with a nervous grin on his face. He was bobbing his head up and down as he moved to unlock the rear door.

'Let's head back to the hotel. Our flights to Faro in southern Portugal leave early in the morning.' Jensen was walking quickly down the dark alleyway, headed for the nearby bustling streets, his right hand always ready to grab his hidden gun in case of trouble. Luna Smythe was one pace behind, her senses on full alert, wondering what lay ahead for them.

Chapter 6

Six months earlier, two members of the Hong Kong-based criminal syndicate, which had been decimated by widespread raids from local and international authorities, had been fortunate to escape. Yen Chow Yu and Ping Xiaoyan were relatively junior members of the syndicate, and neither had been at their home nor at any of the places of business when raided.

Yu and Xiao had implemented their escape strategies and rendezvoused at a remote location in southern China. By agreement, each had gone their own separate ways by private jet, with neither knowing where the other was headed. They met at a prearranged location in Faro in southern Portugal three months later. Yu and Xiao were staying at the Hotel Eva, a four-star hotel on the waterfront adjacent to the marina, overlooking the beautiful Ria Formosa National Park on the southern-most tip of Portugal. The Ria Formosa estuary is comprised of a labyrinth of canals, islands, marshland and sandy beaches. Although in distinct contrast to the azure blue water and picturesque beaches that the remainder of the Algarve coast is renowned for, the estuary offered its own unique beauty.

Yu was a thirty-two-year-old Chinese national who had been groomed from an early age to become an enforcer for the Hong Kong-based criminal syndicate. The syndicate had numerous enforcers at their disposal. The exceptional ones, like Yu, were sometimes invited to become members of the syndicate. Their leader at the time, Adrian Low, had himself been the syndicate's most ruthless and successful assassin. Low was assassinated by long range sniper shot in London six months ago, while in the maximum-security custody of authorities. Yu had a similar imposing physique to Adrian Low, and had worked hard at building his own physique and reputation in the image of Low.

Xiao, on the other hand, was elevated to a seat at the table at the very young age of twenty-nine because of her razor-sharp instincts and incredible knowledge of both their illicit businesses and the intricacies of the syndicate's global money laundering operations.

Yu and Xiao were regarded by all as part of the next generation of the syndicate, although no one expected that they would be elevated to the head of the syndicate at such young ages. That had not stopped either of them. While each had laid low for the first three months, once they reconnected in southern Portugal, they had not wasted any time in their endeavours to piece together the remnants of those who worked for the original syndicate.

Yu poured them each a glass of sangria from the jug on the table in the rooftop bar area of the Hotel Eva, adjacent to the pool. They had just finished their light lunch and taken a brief dip in the heated pool.

'To us and the syndicate.' Yu raised his glass, making no secret of his admiration for Xiao. With her lithe, slim physique, pert breasts and shoulder-length jet black hair, she looked exceptional in her brief black bikini. The ever-present malicious glint in her eyes though, that was another matter entirely.

*

'To us and the syndicate,' Xiao repeated, touching the edge of her glass goblet to his. While Xiao admired Yu's physique, she was not interested in him, or any other male for that matter. Her preferences lay elsewhere. She was also singularly focused on the resurrection of the syndicate and the restoration of it to its former glory. Many, including Yu, did not know that she was the daughter of the syndicate's former leader, Adrian Low. Xiao was also looking to exact revenge on Tom Jackson and Jason Jones, who had not only struck a near-fatal blow to the syndicate, but had also cost her so much personally.

It was Xiao who had kept track of Murray Jensen after his escape from custody. She had remained in close contact with him, and was delighted to hear of his success in South and Central America. Xiao had maintained a macabre interest in Jensen's bloody pursuits and was anxious to reconnect with him in respect to their mutual business activities. The timing of Jensen's new arrangements with the Colombian drug cartel was near perfect. She and Yu were also ready to ramp up their illegal operations.

In anticipation of Murray Jensen and Luna Smythe's arrival at the hotel sometime before seven that evening, Xiao had booked a table at the locally renowned seafood restaurant at the end of the marina, Marisqueira Faro e Benfica.

*

Jensen and Smythe's journey took them from Quito direct to Madrid, where they passed through security and immigration with ease. As Jensen had said, no one would be on the lookout for a married couple who were Spanish nationals. They had also both been careful to alter their general appearance sufficiently to ensure that they would not be recognised by facial recognition technology in particular. Luna had run numerous computer simulations to verify that their disguises were effective.

The alternative to the direct first leg flight to Madrid had been flights to either Miami in the USA or London. Jensen determined that each of the alternatives carried too much risk. Both the UK and the USA were known to have the most sophisticated facial recognition technology available. He also knew that with the route he had selected, their passports would only need to be checked once as they entered the European Union. From Madrid they flew to Lisbon and then on to Faro in southern Portugal. There were extra layover time periods with the flights he had chosen, but he reasoned it was worth it to avoid unnecessary risks.

Murray Jensen slept for most of the time they were flying. He did not wish to socialise with Luna Smythe, and particularly not after her comments in Quito when she had seen the passports represented them as a married couple. He was attracted to Luna, but was well aware from experience just how much focus could be lost when personal relationships encroached on the work environment.

'You might be wondering why we didn't fly in the private jet,' he said absentmindedly to Luna as their flight was on final approach to the Faro airport.

'Not really. I'm sure there's a good reason, and you are after all the head honcho, hunneybun.' Luna added the final comment both as a tease to Jensen, and to keep up the public appearance of a married couple.

Jensen did not take the bait. He knew exactly what she was doing. 'The private jet will never be far away from us, in case we need it.' He had directed the pilot to relocate the jet somewhere safe and untraceable within the European Union, and within one hour's flight time from wherever they were. Jensen was always planning for contingencies.

Chapter 7

Tom Jackson's Qantas flight left Brisbane International Airport just before nine p.m. His total trip time to Rome was twenty-five hours, including a three-and-a-half-hour layover in Dubai. With the time difference of nine hours, his scheduled arrival at Fiumicino airport in Rome was one p.m. on Thursday.

Jackson spent most of Wednesday in the office meeting with his client to discuss the documentation. To their surprise, a second Terms Sheet had been presented to them in the morning. Tom was instructed to focus on the first Terms Sheet since that buyer had engaged lawyers in London who had already had input into the document. He was to nevertheless progress the second Terms Sheet in parallel, as a backup. The second document had been prepared by one of the selling agents, and would require a significant redraft by Tom before it could be presented to the second buyer and their advisors.

Jackson and his client settled on further changes to the first Terms Sheet, and Tom emailed the revised version to the London lawyers. They gave way on many of the pedantic changes requested by the London lawyer, simply because it was at no cost to them in a commercial sense, and was also the path of least resistance. Tom warned the client, however, that it did not bode well for the negotiation of the primary transaction documents. He had dealt with that type of lawyer on many occasions, and had always been careful to ensure that the give and take in the negotiations was not glaringly one-sided. Jackson was skilful at allowing opposing lawyers to pontificate, but never to the detriment of the commercial outcomes for his client. The intended optimum result was to achieve the client's preferred outcomes and allow opposing counsel to maintain an inflated level of self-importance, which in turn translated into a strong recommendation to their client to move forward. It was a delicate balancing act that Jackson was very good at. He was regularly complimented by his clients for leaving his own ego out of the equation.

Tom worked on the second Terms Sheet while in the Qantas business lounge at the airport. He emailed his preliminary redraft and associated comments to his client before pouring his second glass of French champagne. Time to relax and enjoy the trip, Tom told himself.

While in the past he hardly ever travelled overseas without being accompanied by his now estranged wife, Mary, he reluctantly admitted to himself that he was becoming accustomed to travelling on his own. He selected the latest Ken Follett novel on his Kindle, and allowed himself to relax a little. *A Column of Fire* was the third book in the successful church builder series, set in the mid-sixteenth century in the mythical town of Kingsbridge in south-western England. It had been ten years since Follet had released book two in the series, *World Without End*, and Tom was looking forward to immersing himself in another of Follett's well-researched and engaging novels. Reading was not only an integral part of Jackson's day-to-day professional activities, but it also provided his greatest means of relaxation and escape.

*

While Tom Jackson's flight was roughly half-way to Dubai, Murray Jensen and Luna Smythe arrived at the Hotel Eva in Faro. Jensen and Smythe occupied adjoining rooms on level 4 just below the rooftop pool and bar areas. Their rooms overlooked the multitude of boats in the marina. Sunset was not far off, and Jensen couldn't help noticing the manner in which the evening light showcased the crowded marina and the vast open spaces of the Ria Formosa National Park. His eyes were drawn to the variety of colours and textures afforded by the park's varied landscape.

'We have arrived.' Jensen returned his attention to the hotel handset he was holding. He had been waiting to be connected to Ping Xiaoyan.

'On time as usual,' Xiao responded. 'I have booked a table at the seafood restaurant at the end of the marina, Marisqueira Faro e Benfica, for seven p.m. It's a short walk through the marina, and the seafood there is spectacular. If it's not too soon after your arrival, Yu and I will meet you there.'

'I can see it in the distance. Looks very local. No, not too soon. We've been travelling for a while and have not had a lot to eat over the last several hours. I'm famished. I'm pretty certain Luna is in the same boat. We'll meet you there soon.'

The restaurant was indeed very local. The entrance to it was almost hidden amongst the various boatsheds and other buildings that supported the local fishing industry. While there were tourists at some of the tables, many were populated by what appeared to be local families.

Jensen and Smythe were greeted at the entrance by a grinning maître d' wearing a long white apron. His bushy handlebar moustache amplified his grin, and his large paunch moved up and down as he spoke.

'Buenas noches, good evening. Bienvenidos, welcome wonderful people.' The maître d' spoke in Spanish, rather than Portuguese, as many tourists struggled with the Portuguese language.

'I can see our friends are already here.' Jensen rudely dismissed the effervescent waiter, who shrugged his shoulders and stepped aside to let Jensen and Smythe pass.

As they approached the table, Yu and Xiao rose as one. As Jensen took Xiao's outstretched hand, he noticed both the deceptive strength in her grip and her cold, heartless brown eyes. He made a mental note not to underestimate this one. There was also something very familiar about her, which he set aside in his mind to explore at a later time.

'Nice to finally meet you in person, Murray,' Ping Xiaoyan said quietly to Jensen in a monotone voice, as she released her grip on his hand. Jensen could see that she was outwardly smiling and at the same time sizing him up.

'And you, Xiao. I've heard a great deal about you.' Jensen watched her intently as she tilted her head. He was reminded of cobra poised to strike. His attention was distracted by the other person who had been awaiting their arrival.

'Honoured to meet you, Senor Sanchez.' Yen Chow Yu had adopted an upright stance with his feet almost touching each other and his head slightly bowed.

'The pleasure is mine, Yu.' *Curious*, Jensen thought to himself. *Yu is the ruthless assassin and yet he has toed the line by showing respect and making use of my alias. I see that he clearly has the killer instinct, and yet that pales into insignificance when compared to the ruthless aura surrounding Xiao.*

Luna Smythe had greeted both Yu and Xiao, and all were taking their seats.

The portly waiter appeared as soon as the last of them was seated, carrying two huge fish. He had one in each hand, holding them up by the gills. Even with his arms held out horizontally, the tail of each fish was touching the floor. 'Bacalhau, our special cod and one of the most popular fishes in the Portuguese cuisine,' he said jovially by way of explanation. 'May I recommend these two beautiful fishes to you. The chef knows exactly how to cook and serve these to you. I assure you that you will not be disappointed.'

As the group looked at each other to see what each thought of the idea, another waiter set a huge platter in the centre of the table. On it was all manner of seafood including octopus, prawns and a variety of shellfish. Some was cooked, but most was in its natural state.

Jensen was impressed, and looked at the head waiter and nodded. 'Impressive. Bring local wine to match.'

'Si senor.' The waiter involuntarily wriggled, which caused his protruding belly to move comically from side to side. 'Afterwards we will have port, the national drink of Portugal,' he called over his shoulder as he hurried away.

'It's been a long day. Why don't we enjoy the evening and meet up in a more private location tomorrow morning to discuss next steps,' Jensen said, in his means-business tone, leaving little room for debate.

Chapter 8

DAY 4 (Thursday)

Jackson's flight landed at the Fiumicino airport in Rome shortly after one p.m. local time. By the time he collected his luggage, made his way through customs and immigration, and took a taxi ride to his hotel in central Rome, it was a little after 2:30 p.m.

Tom had stayed at the Colonna Palace Hotel in Via della Colonna Antonina on several occasions. It was centrally located and adjacent to the Palazzo Montecitorio, which was the seat of the Chamber of Deputies, the lower house of the Italian Parliament. It was a vibrant part of the city. There was always some protest or other taking place at the locked iron gates protecting the parliamentary precinct, necessitating a permanent and extensive police presence.

The historic building housing the hotel had been luxuriously restored, and room sizes were unexpectedly generous for a European building of its age. The garden restaurant on top of the five-level building, where a delicious breakfast was served every morning, afforded a view of surrounding historical houses and shops dating back to the sixteenth century. The hotel was within walking distance of some of Rome's most enchanting historical sites, including the Pantheon, Trevi Fountain, the Spanish Steps and Piazza Navona. Tom knew that he could also walk to the Colosseum in around thirty minutes.

After checking in at reception, Jackson headed for his room to freshen up. Next stop was the beautiful roof garden to take in the sights and generally soak up the atmosphere of all that was Rome. He took out his mobile phone and dialled Lorenzo Bassutri's number.

'Ciao, Signor Tom. Have you arrived in beautiful Roma already?'

'Si, Lorenzo. I'm at the Colonna Palace Hotel.'

'Ah, a magnifico hotel. Very central.'

'Can we meet up this afternoon, Lorenzo?'

'Of course. What time works for you.'

'Would around six be suitable?'

'Assolutamente, absolutely. I am sure you know this already, but our office is located in Via Po, not far from Villa Borghese. It's about ten minutes in the taxi from your hotel.'

'Grazie, Lorenzo. That will give me time to have a look around at some of the nearby sites and have a rest before we meet up.'

'Prego, you're welcome, Tom. We can have a meal together after our meeting.'

'Sounds excellent. See you around six.'

Jackson wasted no time in heading out to enjoy the busy cobblestoned streets. His first stop was the Trevi Fountain, where tourists of all ages thronged the picturesque setting, taking selfies. Then on to the marvel that is the Pantheon. Originally built as a Roman temple around two thousand years ago, the Pantheon had served as a Catholic church since AD 609. Tom had been inside the Pantheon many times, and each time he was in awe at the world's largest unreinforced dome. He knew that it was one of the best-preserved of all ancient Roman buildings. Tourists crowded the interior, with most craning their necks upward to observe the central opening to the sky.

Fatigue from his long flight was beginning to set in, and he resolved to save other sites such as the Colosseum for another day. He headed for nearby Piazza Navona, one of his favourite places in the world, for a coffee and chocolate croissant. He selected a table outside facing the three famous travertine fountains in the centre of the piazza. Although it was mid- spring, the weather was not too cold to sit outside and soak up the atmosphere. There was always music, with many of the buskers moving from café to café to serenade patrons and collect donations. Tom had brought a selection of coins with him solely for this purpose.

Deep in his own thoughts and sipping a double espresso, Jackson suddenly became more alert. The hairs on the back of his neck were prickling. Were those two staring at him, or was that his imagination? He locked eyes with what at first glance appeared to be a tourist couple, and each immediately disengaged from their observation of him. It was a subtle reflex action for both of them, but it didn't go unnoticed by Jackson. His Krav Maga training had taught him to be on alert for any kind of threat.

*

That morning in Faro, southern Portugal, Murray Jensen, Luna Smythe, Yen Chow Yu and Ping Xiaoyan had opted for an early meeting over breakfast on the rooftop of the Hotel Eva. There was no one else within hearing range.

'Where are you at with things, Xiao?' Jensen intentionally directed his query to Xaio, who was clearly the higher intellect of the two from China. To his credit, Yu was happy to defer to Xiao on financial matters. Instead, he kept a watchful eye to ensure they were aware as soon as anyone was close enough to hear their conversation.

'A suitable transaction in Italy has been referred to us. The asset price is €200 million and we were struggling to gather together sufficient funds within the tight time frame demanded by the seller. Your timing is perfect, Luis.' Jensen was pleased that Xiao was careful to use his alias while speaking openly in public. 'Would your connections be able to make up the €50 million we are short?'

'No.' Jensen's prompt negative response surprised both Xiao and Yu. He continued before either spoke. 'My brief is to provide the entire asset price, so long as it is within a prearranged limit, which it is. That is non-negotiable, I'm afraid. The cartel must own the entire asset. You will, of course, be appropriately rewarded with a twelve per cent facilitation fee.'

Jensen could see that Xiao was struggling with the concept. He knew that in the past the syndicate had only laundered their own monies. Laundering a third party's funds was a first for them.

'Fifteen per cent.' Xiao said, seemingly without a great deal of thought, although Jensen could see that she had razor-sharp focus. He was certain she would see that €30 million will help their cause. *Those eyes*, he thought again to himself.

'Done.' Jensen had been authorised to offer up to fifteen per cent commission.

'You will need to put me in touch with your connection's financial people so I can begin arranging the logistics.'

'No problem. I do know that the cartel's funds on this occasion will come from their numbered Swiss bank accounts, the same place where I understand yours were to be sourced. That way, you should be able to utilise near identical procedures to the ones you were already planning.'

Jensen saw Xiao visibly relax a little, and when she did, so too did Yen Chow Yu.

*

Tom Jackson finished the remainder of his coffee and croissant, and headed back to his hotel. He used only main roads and pathways, just to be safer. He kept a constant vigilance to see if he could again spot his observers. He did not.

Once in the privacy of his hotel room, he dialled Jason Jones' number. Five p.m. in Rome equated to two a.m. in Sydney, and he was hoping Jones would not mind being disturbed at that hour given the circumstances. He wasn't.

'Tom. Everything okay?'

'I'm not sure, Jason. Sorry to disturb you so early. But I'm certain I caught a couple disguised as tourists surveilling me in Piazza Navona. When I locked eyes with them, they each looked away at exactly the same time. It was subtle but definitely not a coincidence. I don't know what to make of it.'

'Nor do I yet, mate. Do you have any details of the buyer or their financier?'

'Not yet,' Tom replied, feeling more relaxed than he probably should.

'Can you get me on the payroll for this deal with your client? I'll the reach out to Oliver Planksmith in London and ask him to send someone over pronto to keep an eye on you. He's a lot closer than I am.'

Oliver Planksmith had served with Jones on two of his three tours to Afghanistan. The British and Australian special forces units had worked in very close cooperation. They were brothers in arms, and it was Jones who had encouraged Oliver to set up his business after leaving the army. He had a successful private security business in the United Kingdom that enjoyed a reputation similar to that of Jones' business. Planksmith and his operatives had been integral to all that had taken place in London and Cairo six months ago.

'Thanks, and will do. I may be jumping at shadows... but I don't think so.'

'Your instincts are honed, Tom. Don't doubt yourself. I'll get someone there as soon as I can.'

After the call ended, Jackson made contact with his client, who had no issues with bringing Jason Jones on board to provide security for Tom. It was a sad indictment of society that all functioning at this level of finance were quick to recognise that criminal elements were lurking in the shadows at every turn.

Jackson sent a quick email message to Jones, who responded promptly to confirm he would get in touch with Oliver and revert to Tom with arrangements.

Chapter 9

After a brief rest, Jackson walked to the office of Andrich Wiley, about half an hour away in Via Po.

Lorenzo Bassutri greeted Tom in the well-appointed reception area.

'Signor Tom. Lovely to meet you in person. Your reputation precedes you.'

'As does yours,' Jackson replied politely as he shook Bassutri's proffered hand.

'This way,' Lorenzo beckoned, as he turned on his black patent shoes and headed for a nearby meeting room. He was wearing a tailored navy suit with a white open-necked shirt underneath. Lorenzo was in his late thirties, quite young for a partner in a global law firm with a reputation such as his. His jet-black hair was slicked back on his head with hair gel. A pair of spectacles with a blood-red frame were propped on his generous nose.

Jackson was shown into a meeting room with a mahogany table and matching chairs for eight. Original paintings depicting different iconic sites throughout Italy adorned two of the walls. Each of the other two walls was glass from ceiling to floor. One was frosted glass and faced the reception area, and the other looked out over the magnificent Villa Borghese Gardens.

'Impressive, Lorenzo.' Tom turned his attention away from the window and took a seat. 'You live in a very special city.'

'I know, and I have promised myself never to take it for granted.'

'Very wise. Would you like me to give you a verbal update on how things have progressed since the brief I sent to you a couple of days ago?' Bassutri nodded and Jackson continued. 'As you know from my email to the London lawyers, which I copied to you, we've made progress with the Terms Sheet. We conceded a few points, but nothing of any real significance. Once we agree on and sign the Terms Sheet, I would like be in a position to deliver the first draft of the primary transaction documents. I have a preliminary draft and would like to work on that with you over the next twenty-four to forty-eight hours to get your input from a local perspective. I've done a few of these deals for this client, although never one in Italy. My client-approved base documents will be a good starting point for us.'

'I expected that would be our next steps. Can you let me have your drafts, and I'll get to work on them straight away.' Lorenzo was alert and smiling. Tom could see that the lawyer was as passionate about this type of work as he was.

'Will do. Can you ask your team to undertake detailed searches of the buyer entity and of those with any underlying interests?'

They spent the next hour and a half talking through the specifics of the Terms Sheet and the draft primary transaction documents. Both acknowledged that there was work to be done on the primary documents. They could start that process in earnest now that they were close on the Terms Sheet. While not binding on the parties, the Terms Sheet was designed to be an accurate guide to both the key terms in the primary documents as well as the process to negotiate them.

'One added complication is that we have received a second Terms Sheet with slightly inferior terms. The client has asked me to keep that confidential for now. I will continue to progress that document separately. It is to be the backup in the event the first deal falters for any reason.'

Lorenzo had pre-booked a table at a nearby two-Michelin star restaurant for eight p.m. He had also pre-ordered.

'I hope you like seafood, Tom. I should have checked, sorry.'

'Certainly do.' Tom was ravenous. He hadn't had much to eat since the plane trips, during which he'd been provided with no fewer than five meals.

The first course was a reef fish ceviche. The main course was something to behold. Lorenzo explained to Tom that this dish was a specialty of the restaurant, and usually had to be ordered twenty-four hours in advance. The waiter appeared with a large capped earthen-ware pot. He carefully removed the cap and began tipping the pot to pour out its contents. Marinated seafood of all shapes and sizes gently slid from the pot into the large empty bowls in front of each of them, accompanied by a tomato-based chowder. Tom could make out octopus, squid, clams and multiple different types of both pink and white fish pieces. Large chunks of warm garlic bread had also been delivered to their side plates.

They sat in near total silence while they consumed the exquisite meal.

'Unbelievably delicious meal, grazzie mille, Lorenzo. I enjoyed every single mouthful. Great choice.'

'Prego, you're welcome, Signor Tom.'

'It's getting late, and I'm a little fatigued from my travels. Thanks again for the meal, Lorenzo. Shall we meet up in your office at ten a.m. tomorrow?' Bassutri nodded his agreement.

As it was late, Tom decided to catch an Uber ride to his hotel. He had not seen anyone remotely suspicious since Piazza Navona, but that did not mean he was not being watched.

*

'Are you certain you were both spotted?' Matteo Ricci was furious and pacing back and forward in his small office in central Rome.

'Si boss, sorry.' Dante Lombordo responded for both himself and his sister Caterina, slouching lower in his chair as he lowered his chin to his chest.

'Stupido.' Ricci thumped his fist on the desk, his eyes bulging. 'You are my best at surveillance. Explain yourselves.'

Matteo Ricci was the head of operations for the Sicilian mafia in Rome, and was not one to be trifled with. He had literally fought his way to the top of the organisation to earn that position. He was fifty-five and had no intention of retiring. Ricci ruled with an iron fist. To some he might look a little overweight. To those who knew him, however, he was the ultimate strong man. You underestimated him at your peril. At six foot two, his imposing bulk allowed him to intimidate most just by glaring at them with his hooded blue-grey eyes. Most within the organisation cowered before him, and those who did not were generally persuaded to do so by other more physical means.

'Let me explain, boss,' Dante stammered. 'We have kept an eye on Tom Jackson since his arrival earlier today, as ordered. We were careful to keep our distance while he was on the move. When he settled in to relax in a café in Piazza Navona, we were confident that we could do the same. It was only for a split second that he looked in our direction, and I knew straight away that he had spotted us. It was like he was almost asleep one minute, and then suddenly he was transformed into a predator, his instincts on high alert. He must have some kind of training.'

'I have been told he is trained in a form of martial arts, although I am not sure which one. I can't spare anyone else at the moment to track Jackson's whereabouts. I'm not yet sure of the significance of doing so, but our Chinese client was adamant that we keep an eye on him. I will report to her that so far all he has done is sightsee and meet with an Italian lawyer. You two don't let him out of your sight. Work in shifts if need be, and report to me every two hours.' Ricci scowled and pointed to the door.

The brother and sister scuttled out of Ricci's office, like the cockroaches they were.

After they had left his office, Ricci dialled Ping Xiaoyan's cell phone. 'Buonasera, good evening, Xiao. It's Matteo. We have kept Signor Jackson under surveillance since his arrival, as you have requested. Nothing out of the ordinary so far. Some sightseeing and a meeting with a lawyer from Andrich Wiley. He's back at his hotel now.' Matteo had not met Xiao or her travelling companion Yen Chow Yu, but his instincts warned him not to admit to any kind of failure, however insignificant it might seem. He knew all about the Hong Kong-based syndicate they were part of and was aware of the unfortunate fate of the other syndicate members. They were a powerful global organisation, and raids by authorities six months ago would have caused nothing more than a brief pause and pivot in direction.

'Alright, Matteo. I need to meet with you in person tomorrow. There has been a slight change in plans. I can get an early flight to Rome from Faro in Portugal. Arrival time is early afternoon. Let's meet at your office around three p.m.'

'Bene, fine. My office is at the southern end of Via Cassia, right at the intersection with Via degli Orti della Farnesina, not far from the River Tiber. I'll send you a link.'

'I'll find it. See you then.' Xaio ended the call abruptly.

*

Ping Xaioyan dialled Murray Jensen's secure cell phone. 'It's Xiao. I'm travelling to Rome in the morning to meet with a contact to rearrange things a little to accommodate the altered source of funds.'

'Stay in touch.' Jensen looked at his phone after Xiao had disconnected. That was to be expected, he told himself, although he wondered to himself what contact Xiao might have in Rome. He might workshop that with Smythe in the morning.

Chapter 10

Jackson enjoyed a sumptuous breakfast in the rooftop garden area of his hotel. The continental breakfast was more than adequate. A variety of fresh fruit, all manner of breads and croissants baked in the hotel's kitchen, and freshly made barista coffee. The cloudless blue sky lightened his mood as he thought about the day ahead.

He rose early so that he could enjoy the rooftop breakfast and then walk over to the Colosseum for a quick tour. That would leave sufficient time to return to the hotel to change and catch an uber ride to his ten a.m. meeting with Lorenzo Bassutri.

Tom had visited the Colosseum twice in the past. Between his first and second visits, the site curators had excavated more of its history, and had at the same time added subtle modern enhancements to improve both the safety of the site and the means for visitors to enjoy it. This visit was no different. There was more to see, and the viewing platform in the centre had been extended to allow visitors to look down into the arena and surrounding corridors through which the gladiators had entered. Tom experienced the same surreal feeling he had on each of his two prior visits. He would have loved to share the experience with Ros Green. Ros had been the chair of the board of directors of Tom's client. She was brutally murdered in London by agents of the Hong Kong-based criminal syndicate twelve short months ago. Tom and Ros

48

had struck up a romantic relationship while in London, attempting to expose the truth about the syndicate's involvement in a real estate development Ros's company was undertaking in Brisbane. The sad memory of Ros reminded him of the need for vigilance.

Jackson left the central viewing platform and climbed high on one side of the Colosseum when he absentmindedly noticed a tour group assembling lower down on the opposite side. To his amusement they began chanting 'Maximus, Maximus, Maximus.' *Gladiator*, in which Australian actor Russell Crowe played the Academy Award winning role of Maximus, was one of Tom's all-time favourite movies. He had goosebumps on his arms as he heard the chant rise above the central arena. His attention was drawn to one in the group who looked to be part of it, but was not chanting with the rest.

They're still watching me, he thought to himself. The person not chanting was without doubt the male of the pair he'd caught watching him the day before in the Piazza Navona. He looked around briefly but was unable to spot the female member of the surveillance team.

Jackson left the Colosseum and headed for his hotel, certain that he would be followed. Reflecting on his call the day before with Jason Jones, he reminded himself of Jason's email overnight that Oliver Planksmith was sending someone from his organisation to provide security for him. He was to meet up with them at his hotel around one for lunch. He allowed himself to relax a little, and at the same time remained on alert for any sign of an immediate threat. He also started to speculate why he'd have a tail on him in Rome. What was he getting himself into with this deal – or was his tail even connected to the deal?

His priority for now was to focus on his meeting with Lorenzo Bassutri.

'Buongiorno, Lorenzo,' Jackson greeted Bassutri, who motioned him towards the same meeting room as the day before.

'Tom, I would like you to meet a senior member of my team, Francesca Obliti. Francesca, this is the famous Tom Jackson.'

'Signor Jackson, it's an absolute pleasure to meet you. I have read extensively about your career and in particular your, shall I say, exploits over the last couple of years,' Francesca said in a quiet businesslike voice with an outstretched hand, her clear green eyes maintaining direct eye contact with Tom's.

'The pleasure is mine, I'm sure.' Jackson took her outstretched hand, as she smiled broadly, displaying perfectly even white teeth.

Bassutri had already taken a seat at the mahogany table, and Tom and Francesca followed his lead. Tom sat opposite the two of them, facing the picturesque view over the Villa Borghese Gardens.

'I have made good progress overnight with your primary documents, Tom, adding only those provisions I consider essential to deal with local jurisdictional and other matters. As you said yesterday, your client-approved base documents are an excellent starting point. Perhaps we can work through my changes in general terms and you can have a look at them in more detail later.'

'Sounds good, Lorenzo.'

'Before we get into the specifics of the documents, I'll let Francesca tell you how the searches of the buyer have progressed.'

Francesca tabled a large number of printed searches and spoke about each one in turn.

'Grazie, Francesca,' Tom said after she had completed her overview of the searches. 'So the bottom line is that your searches have not revealed anything out of the ordinary. The buyer is a new entity recently incorporated in London, with legitimate London-based agents. You have not been able to trace the underlying ownership structure beyond the first level, which also looks to be legitimate.'

'Correct, Tom. Our further searches of beneficial ownership interests have encountered the usual sophisticated security and privacy protocols employed by the Swiss banking system. I have seen this before, as I am sure you have, and do not see anything to be concerned about. It is not as if we are dealing with an entity from one of the notorious Caribbean Island tax havens.' Francesca was gathering her searches and stacking them in a neat pile. As she looked up, she casually flicked her long shiny brown hair behind her slender shoulders. 'I will email copies of all searches to you for your records.'

'Interesting.' Jackson steepled his hands, reflecting on the outcome of the searches. 'It is always a little frustrating not being able to peel all the layers away to expose the true ownership structure, although I do understand the reasons for it. The buyer's London lawyer emailed me overnight to confirm that there will be no third-party financier. This is to effectively be a cash deal, with funds to be provided to the lawyer from Swiss bank accounts. The London lawyer has indicated they are in the process of satisfying themselves from the perspective of the current anti-bribery and corruption laws. I have accepted his offer to share the outcomes of his enquiries, which we will of course need to test.' Lorenzo and Francesca both nodded their agreement.

They spent the next two hours carefully examining the changes that Bassutri and his team had made to the primary documents. Tom was impressed. Lorenzo had kept to the brief and imported only essential provisions to the documents, taking account of Italian laws and other local issues that Tom had not previously been aware of. He had not sought to imprint his own style on the documents.

'Thank you both. This is great progress. I have a meeting soon back at my hotel. After that I'll work through your amendments in more detail, and send the altered documents to my client with my comments and any suggested further amendments. I will copy you both into the email to keep you in the loop. I know it's Saturday tomorrow, but is there any chance we can meet up in the morning to fine tune the documents to take account of my input, as well as any comments from my client overnight? I'd like very much to maintain the momentum in this deal. My client's required time frame is extremely tight. I thought after that we might travel out to the Mondo Dei Sogni theme park. I haven't been to the park before and would like to match up its physical attributes with the written detail my client has provided.'

'No problems, Tom. I can meet you here at ten a.m. again if that works. A trip to the theme park afterwards is a great idea. I can show you around. Francesca, there is no need for you to join us, unless of course you are free and would like to?'

'I am free, and would like to, thank you. I love that place and I am keen to learn from the best everything I can about the processes of an amazing transaction like this one.' Francesca's face lit up with enthusiasm. Her eyes were sparkling and her smile was broader than Tom thought possible.

'Tomorrow it is then.' Tom nodded politely to each as he departed.

Jackson caught a taxi this time back to his hotel. He was annoyed that he could not walk. He loved to walk through any European city, and in particular Rome. Maybe he could do so after he had his security in place. The ten-minute journey to the hotel was insufficient time for any real reflection on the lengthy meeting he'd just had. He would revisit the meeting and the altered documents after he had met with Planksmith's operative over lunch.

*

Willow Douglas was delighted when Oliver Planksmith had selected her to travel to Rome on short notice to provide security for Tom Jackson. Oliver was completely unaware of the intimacies she and Tom had enjoyed after their daring escape from captivity in London last year. Tom almost lost his life in the process. They had managed to reach one of Planksmith's off-books safe houses, and Oliver was the only one who knew of their whereabouts. Both had given in to their physical attraction to each other when pondering their near-death experiences.

In her early thirties, Willow was an extremely fit and capable security operative. Her piercing blue eyes and blonde shoulder-length hair led many to underestimate her abilities, notwithstanding her near six-foot height.

Willow pictured Tom before he walked into the hotel reception. His tall, athletic frame made him look much younger than someone in their mid-forties. He had a sophisticated and confident air about him that she found very attractive. His dark hair, slightly greying at the temples, enhanced his charming nature.

'Hello, Tom.' Willow grinned as Jackson entered the reception to the Colonna Palace Hotel. Jackson took her outstretched hand and the surprised look on his face quickly dissipated, turning into a warm smile.

Chapter 11

Murray Jensen and Luna Smythe met over an early breakfast on the rooftop of the Hotel Eva in Faro.

'I'm a bit surprised that Xiao and Yu have left Portugal so soon. We only arrived two days ago. I guess they do have to make new arrangements given that none of the syndicate's funds will be in play this time. I'm just curious as to why they've had to go to Rome, and who they might be meeting with over there. I don't trust them.' Jensen was pinching his chin as he spoke.

'Likewise. She has shifty eyes, that one. It looked like she was initially unhappy with your suggestion about not using any of the syndicate's money, and then in an instant she seemed happy to accept what you proposed and to promote it as her own idea. She's a quick thinker and definitely has a plan. Should we go and keep an eye on them?'

Jensen turned to Smythe with a look of surprise, which was accompanied by a menacing grin. 'Now you're starting to think like a field agent, Luna. That was my thought exactly. Let's get out of here and pick up their trail in Rome. No need to broadcast that just yet. I'd like to try and get an idea of what they're up to before we let them know we've decided to join them there.'

Jensen and Smythe arrived in Rome around the time Xiao and Yu were meeting with Matteo Ricci. Before departing Portugal, Luna had activated Jensen's extensive secure network and instructed local assets to track the whereabouts of Yen Chow Yu and Ping Xiaoyan. Once they landed, they were provided with details of not only the pair's hotel but of the location of their three p.m. meeting. They hadn't yet identified the person with whom they were meeting but were making progress.

*

Ping Xiaoyan and Yen Chow Yu arrived in Rome with more than sufficient time to check into their hotel and make their meeting with Sicilian mafia boss, Matteo Ricci, at three.

On their flight from Portugal, Xiao reflected on her brief conversation with Murray Jensen. It was too soon to tell Jensen about why she was travelling to Rome, and who she was meeting with. She knew it wouldn't be long before she would have to tell him about the involvement of the mafia, although she had no intention of sharing the actual details of their role in the money laundering process. Not for the first time since Jensen had called her from South America, Xiao wondered what the reactions would be from the Sicilian mafia and the Colombian drug cartel when each found out that the other was involved. In her mind it was entirely plausible that the two natural enemies could function on the same side of this deal. Geographical separation had in the past been the only successful means of keeping the two forces apart. It would be up to her and Jensen to ensure the process ran smoothly. All the more reason to bring Jensen into the loop sooner rather than later.

Then there was Tom Jackson. The London lawyer notified her of his involvement as soon as he had received the first draft of the Terms Sheet from Jackson. While she had asked the mafia to keep an eye on him just in case, Xiao was confident that Jackson would not be able to break through the cloak of legitimacy surrounding this deal.

She had always known that the third-party intermediary money transfer from tax havens, which the syndicate had relied on in the past, was the weak link. That was, after all, the process that had resulted in the syndicate's former leader, her father Adrian Low, personally being in Cairo and London last year. Another reason to keep tabs on Tom Jackson, she reminded herself. *Revenge.*

A chance meeting had connected her with the Sicilian mafia and from there she had learnt about their incredibly valuable connections within the 'respectable' Swiss banking systems. It was a brilliant long-term play. It had taken many years for their connections to rise to appropriate levels within the banking system to enable them a measure of control over funds transfers. The initial presumption of illicit funds when sourced via a Caribbean tax haven was completely removed, shifting the burden of proof back to the recipient of the funds.

She heard from her contact within Andrich Wiley that Jackson's client had received a second Terms Sheet, which Jackson was separately progressing as a back up to her deal. All the more imperative to push ahead as quickly as possible. She made a mental note to contact their London lawyer direct and ask him to tone down his usual egotistical method of document negotiation. While the method sometimes resulted in beneficial outcomes, there was no time for that process on this occasion.

Ping Xiaoyan and Yen Chow Yu introduced themselves to the Sicilian mafia boss and were ushered into a surprisingly small meeting room. 'A pleasure to meet you both.' Matteo Ricci beamed, although his smile was not reflected in his calculating eyes. 'It is a little unusual to meet in person so early in the process, or at all really. You mentioned a change in plans. Care to explain?'

Xiao had considered how to proceed with the discussion and had decided the direct approach was the best. 'The deal is the same – the purchase of the Mondo Dei Sogni theme park for €200 million. The time frame is, however, a little shorter than we initially thought. More on that later. We will not be using any of our funds.'

Ricci crossed his arms and tilted his head with curiosity. Xiao continued before he could speak. 'The source of funds will still be numbered Swiss bank accounts, so your procedures will be the same. Your fee will be slightly less.' She thought it best to get this on the table before she was forced to disclose the ownership of the funds.

'How much less?' Ricci leaned forward and placed the palms of his outstretched arms flat on the table. The gesture was partly to support his imposing bulk, and partly to convey the threat that he was about to leap out of his chair.

Xiao started momentarily, before regaining her composure. She leaned forward, placing her own hands on the table, causing the well-honed muscles in her arms to ripple. She held Ricci's gaze with such deep intensity that he relaxed a little and sat back in his chair. She did likewise. 'Your fee will be five per cent instead of the eight per cent we previously discussed. Take it or leave it.'

Ricci leaned back further and looked up at the ceiling. 'I may well just leave it then.'

'Fine.' Xiao responded quickly and rose to leave, signalling Yu to follow her. She knew it was risky to call his bluff. She was at the same time aware of how important mutual respect was in relationships of this nature.

'Don't be too hasty,' Ricci said in an even tone. 'Sit down both of you. How about seven per cent?'

'Six and a half.'

'Done.' Matteo said after a brief pause, offering his hand to shake on the revised terms.

Xiao smiled inwardly. She had been prepared to pay the full eight percent. The €3 million she had just saved was a pleasant surprise. It also meant that the syndicate's eight and a half per cent commission was symbolically higher that the mafia's six and a half per cent. She made a mental note of that, more for her own personal satisfaction than anything else.

'So whose money is it?' Ricci had been so focused on the commission negotiations his question was almost an afterthought.

'I am working through an intermediary by the name of Murray Jensen,' Xiao began.

'Ah. I have heard of Signor Jensen. Wasn't he caught up in the raids by authorities on your operations last year? I heard he had gone to ground somewhere to lick his wounds. South America possibly?'

'He was, and your information is correct. Jensen has been in South America personally undertaking wetwork for the most powerful of the Colombian drug cartels.'

Ricci's shoulders tensed at the mention of his organisation's arch-rival. 'Are you telling me that the money you require us to launder via Switzerland is Colombian drug cartel money?' His eyes narrowed.

'I am,' Xiao responded calmly. 'Slightly unusual I know, but as I see it, this presents us both with another business opportunity. Is there a problem?'

'Only if those fuckers think they can muscle into our sphere of operations with their product.' Ricci scowled.

'I have been assured by Jensen that this is a remote funds transfer issue only. Nothing else.' She would need to double check with Jensen, although he had not said otherwise.

'Okay then. I will be watching this closely. You will need to provide my finance people with all of the pertinent details.'

'I have that here on an encrypted thumb drive. I will send you the password via our encrypted messaging system.' Satisfied that the deal was now done, Ping Xiaoyan moved on to Tom Jackson. 'So what is the latest with your surveillance on Jackson?'

'He met with the lawyer again this morning and he is now back at his hotel. I had to split my team this morning. One outside Jackson's hotel and another outside his lawyer's office. I wanted to mix it up a little so he didn't spot the surveillance. It looks like Jackson has been joined by a colleague. A tall, good-looking blonde woman.'

'Keep me informed with details of anything out of the ordinary.' Xiao and Yu rose to leave the meeting. She wondered why Ricci seemed a little nervous when describing his surveillance techniques. She also needed to know who the tall blonde woman was.

Chapter 12

Tom Jackson and Willow Douglas spent their time over lunch in the hotel getting reacquainted.

'So you're telling me you've spotted active surveillance both yesterday and today?' Willow had reverted to her role as Jackson's professional protector.

'Yesterday there was a male and female. Their eyes and mannerisms were almost identical. They could well be brother and sister. I only saw the man this morning.'

'Hmm. Doesn't mean she wasn't there,' Willow continued as Jackson nodded his agreement. 'Given the events that took place last year, let's treat them as a credible threat. Are you carrying any kind of weapon, Tom?'

'Just this.' Jackson grinned as he produced a large Swiss army pocket knife. 'I picked this up from one of the street vendors yesterday.'

'I have a spare handgun. Would you like it?'

'No thanks. You keep both, Willow. I prefer to use my body parts as weapons. The knife is a last resort.'

Tom saw a brief smile flicker across Willow's face at his deliberate use of the term 'body parts'. He quickly put aside his thoughts of their steamy encounter in the safe house in London last year. 'Let's find a secure place to call Jason to let him know where things are at and that you have arrived.'

Tom could see the hesitant look in Willow's eyes. She was no doubt thinking he was going to suggest they head to one of their rooms to make the call. 'There's a business meeting room on level one we can use.' Willow seemed to relax, although as she broke eye contact, he thought that her relief may have been tempered by a little disappointment.

'His phone went straight to voicemail. I guess 2:30 p.m. here is 11:30 p.m. in Sydney. A little late, even for Jason. I'll send him a quick email to confirm you have arrived and to let him know that hostile surveillance is continuing.' Jackson opened his Gmail and looked up at Willow. 'Huh! Thinking of the bastard has conjured him up.'

'I beg your pardon?' Willow looked confused.

'Ah, sorry. Just something we say a lot in Aus. I couldn't reach Jason by phone but when I opened my email account there was an unread email from him. It was sent a little over two hours ago and in it he tells me he was about to board an international flight headed for Rome. He'll arrive here in Rome around midday to-morrow. He says he's concerned for my well-being and that he doesn't want me to have all the fun.'

Willow laughed. 'You Aussies are a funny bunch.' Tom loved the way the top of her button nose crinkled when she laughed. 'Let's hope we truly don't need the extra firepower. That said, a protective detail of two is way more effective than one.'

Jackson and Willow decided to head to their separate rooms after Tom explained that he needed a couple of hours to work through the detail of the Italian lawyer's changes to the primary transaction documents. Willow said that she needed the rest after her early start to the day, and made Jackson promise that he would not leave his room unless she accompanied him.

Their rooms were on the same level, on opposite sides of the corridor. Tom was about to unlock the door to his room when he felt a gentle touch on his shoulder. He turned and was met with a passionate kiss from Willow. As she leaned in, she pressed her lithe, sensual body against his. He responded by holding her in a tight embrace and continuing the kiss with equal passion. Without a word between them, Tom opened his door and they fell onto the bed grasping at each other's clothing. Like two young lovers, they quickly disrobed and engaged in what could only be described as a frenzied love making. Their passionate encounter in London the previous year was not forgotten as they took their activities to the next level. Afterwards, they lay on the bed panting, bathed in perspiration.

'Time for my rest now.' Willow grinned wickedly as she stood to gather her clothing. She wrapped herself in a towel before winking and leaving. 'Catch you later.'

Tom took a shower and spent the rest of the afternoon compiling an email to his client with comments and suggested amendments to the primary documents. He also noted that the Terms Sheet was almost finalised and could likely be signed by both parties early next week.

*

By late afternoon, Murray Jensen's henchmen had learnt that Ping Xiaoyan and Yen Chow Yu had met with Matteo Ricci, who was head of operations in Rome for the Sicilian mafia.

'Fucking unbelievable.' Jensen's lips curled into a snarl as he turned to Luna Smythe, who raised her eyebrows. 'Our Chinese connections are in Rome meeting with the local boss of the Sicilian mafia.'

Smythe wisely kept silent and waited for Jensen to continue his rant.

'Not only that, a pair from the mafia's offices has been spotted surveilling someone. I need to confront Xiao to ask her exactly what the fuck is going on here.' Luna nodded meekly.

Jensen dialled Ping Xiaoyan's cell phone, using their previously agreed secure mode of contact.

'Ah, Murray. I wasn't far off calling to share the latest information with you.' Xiao answered her phone promptly, speaking in her now familiar clipped tone.

This ought to be good, thought Jensen. He remained silent, exercising his better judgement to give Xiao an opportunity to tell her side of the story. He was not expecting to hear the truth.

'Yen Chow Yu and I met this afternoon with Matteo Ricci, the head of operations in Rome for the Sicilian mafia. The phone is on speaker, and Yu can hear both sides of this conversation. No one else can hear us.'

'Likewise on my end, Xiao. Luna is with me,' Jensen said quickly, not wishing to interrupt Xiao for too long.

'Good. I have a confidential arrangement with Ricci and his organisation to assist with the laundering of all funds originating from private Swiss bank accounts. I don't need to share their methodology with you. In fact, I can't. None of the mafia's funds will be involved in the deal we are working together on, and we are sharing our fifteen per cent fee with them.'

'I'm sure you are aware that the Sicilian mafia are arch-rivals of my Colombian drug cartel client?' Jensen said forcefully, the anger and surprise registering in his voice.

'Of course,' Xiao snapped. 'Just hear me out.' Xiao continued in the absence of any response from Jensen. 'I see no reason why both parties cannot on this occasion be on the same side. Your client provides the money, and I facilitate its conversion into a valuable asset. I get paid an agreed fee and I share that with my contacts how I best see fit. My contacts are fine with the proposed arrangements, so long as yours are not seeking to move into their long-held and exclusive territories.' Xiao intentionally emphasised the word *exclusive*. 'Can I assume that is not their plan and that this is a simple funds transfer from a distance?'

Jensen looked at Smythe, who shrugged her shoulders and nodded. 'That is exactly what it is. I will need to make full disclosure to my client, of course. I've not heard anything that might interfere with the détente the parties in question currently enjoy.'

'Of course,' Xiao responded quickly.

Jensen thought he heard exhalation of breath from Ping Xiaoyan. It sounded to him like the truth so far. He decided to reciprocate and tell her of their whereabouts, and also to query the details on the surveillance. 'Luna and I are in Rome.' He let those words hang in the air a little, before continuing, 'We decided this morning that we should join you to lend any required assistance. My sources have already informed me that you were meeting with Matteo Ricci, and we know exactly who he is. Thank you for your candid explanation of the situation.'

'No less than what any serious business colleagues would demand of each other, I'm sure.' Jensen could hear that Xiao was unable to hide the surprise in her voice, nor her admiration for his instincts and resourcefulness.

'Is there anything else you would like to tell me?' Jensen tensed.

Xiao looked at Yu before responding. He shrugged his shoulders with a blank look on his face. 'I don't think so. Perhaps now that we are both in Rome, we can meet up tomorrow.'

'What about the surveillance? Who are the clumsy Mafia goons following and why?' Jensen's words escaped through clenched teeth.

'That is something else I was going to tell you about when we next met,' Xiao lied.

'Bullshit, Xiao. What's going on?'

'Tom Jackson is in Rome. The theme park is owned by his Australian client and Jackson is in town to work on the deal with the Rome office of a well-respected global law firm, Andrich Wiley.' Xiao waited for Jensen to respond.

Jensen was experiencing multiple emotions all at once. Betrayal: How long had Xiao known of Jackson's involvement? Fear: Would Jackson work his fucking magic again and unravel his best chance yet to repair his damaged reputation? Anger mixed with macabre excitement: Tom Jackson and Jason Jones had cost him so much, and here he was presenting his head on the chopping block for the taking. The only thing that could make it any better would be if Jones was also in Rome so that he could exact his merciless revenge on both at the same time.

Jensen's thought processes had provided him with sufficient time to calm down and remind himself that he was not on a free-lance mission in his own interests. He had a very powerful client to keep happy, and he needed to work with Ping Xiaoyan and Yen Chow Yu to achieve that. 'Let's meet at your hotel in the morning at nine to discuss these issues further. Message me the details.' Jensen ended the call before he said anything he might regret.

Chapter 13

Tom Jackson and Willow Douglas decided to walk to the offices of Andrich Wiley. Apart from the fact that it was a lovely spring day in Rome, Willow said that she wanted to see if she could spot their tail. They intentionally detoured slightly on the way and visited Trevi Fountain. It gave them a chance to stop and mingle with the crowd, while each kept a lookout for the pair Jackson had spotted watching him.

Willow touched Tom on the shoulder lightly, tilting her head back slightly as if to laugh. 'At your ten o'clock,' she said quietly out of the side of her mouth. 'That woman in the turquoise crew neck sweater has been in the same spot for too long and seems to have taken an interest in us.'

Without moving his head, Tom allowed his eyes to move to his left. 'I think we have seen what we came here to see. I'm sure there is more to observe, perhaps on the way to our destination.'

'Copy that.' Willow Douglas had been in the armed forces and was well aware that Jackson's language confirmed he had positively identified the woman. Willow took Tom's cue, and they turned to leave together.

With their backs to the woman watching them, Willow continued, 'She has been cleverly ensuring there is always at least one person between her and us, avoiding any obvious direct line of sight.'

'Knowing what she looks like will make it easier for you to spot her male counterpart. As I mentioned, he has very similar facial features and mannerisms. They are likely siblings,' Tom responded.

'Got him,' Willow said almost immediately. 'No need to look. He's just off to the right, wearing a white polo shirt under a light green windcheater. I must say it's not very professional to have a surveillance team comprised of siblings. That said, sometimes it can be a good way to blend in with the crowds of tourists. My guess is that they are low-level henchmen for their organisation, with little or no professional training. Best not to underestimate them though.'

Jackson and Douglas headed off towards the Andrich Wiley office in Via Po for their ten a.m. meeting with Lorenzo Bassutri. Tom was certain their tails would be following. He noticed a slight change in Willow's demeanour. She was on high alert and moved on the balls of her feet, seemingly ready for anything. His own senses were heightened, and his right hand moved to his jacket pocket to confirm the reassuring presence of the Swiss army pocket knife.

They arrived at the office of Andrich Wiley without incident.

'Buongiorno, Lorenzo and Francesca. I'd like you to meet my colleague Willow Douglas who has joined me from London,' Tom said confidently as Lorenzo Bassutri and Francesca Obliti met him and Willow in their reception area.

Lorenzo beamed with delight as he shook the hand of the tall, athletic blonde woman. 'A pleasure to meet you, Signora Willow.'

Francesca offered her greeting to Willow with an undisguised expression bordering on sullen resentment.

Tom ignored the interaction and suggested to Lorenzo that they resume their review of the primary documents. 'My client has provided feedback overnight on your amendments. They are mostly happy with the further amendments I suggested to them.

They do have a few changes that they would like to add in before the documents are sent to the buyer's London lawyer. I've brought my laptop with the latest version of the documents, showing all changes tracked in red. Assuming your hardware is Apple compatible, can I screen-mirror my laptop display with your smart screen on the wall, Lorenzo? We can then work through each amendment together. Willow can make any edits in a different-coloured text for my client's benefit.' Tom allocated the practical task to Willow so that she would not quickly be exposed as a non-lawyer. They had discussed this before the meeting, and both had agreed it was not necessary to disclose that Willow was a highly trained security operative.

'Great idea, Tom.' Lorenzo was reaching for the Samsung remote to the wall screen. 'Compatibility is not an issue.'

They spent most of the next three hours discussing and tweaking the documents in the context of the latest raft of changes by Tom and his client. The process was punctuated by several coffee breaks, which allowed them all to stretch their legs. By the time they had completed the document run-through, all agreed that they were close to a final version that could be sent to the buyer's London lawyers shortly after the signing of the Terms Sheet. Jackson emailed the document to his client, together with a brief email pointing out the further amendments, and recommending acceptance of this version for submission to the other lawyers.

'Great job everyone.' Tom bowed his head slightly in gratitude. 'Now for the fun part. Let's head to the theme park for our tour. This is one of the best parts of working for this client. Theme parks are usually filled to the brim with happy, thrill-seeking patrons.'

'I have the firm's limousine and driver waiting out front for us. Adiamo, let's go,' Bassutri said with a hint of pride, leading the way.

'Impressive! Lead on,' Jackson replied, smiling.

On their way to the Mondo Dei Sogni theme park, they stopped off at a trendy Italian café not far from Piazza Navona, for a light lunch. The cobblestone streets were busier than they had been during the week. Jackson was in his element, soaking up the sights and sounds on offer from their vantage point at the entrance to an alleyway lined with similar businesses. The Italians were so animated when they spoke, gesticulating with their hands and arms to emphasise their words.

Their driver returned when summoned by Lorenzo, and they made their way through the ebbs and flows of the busy city traffic. The theme park was just beyond the outskirts of the city, and they arrived shortly after 2:30 p.m.

Entry to the theme park was by way of the staff entrance, just off to the side of the main entrance for patrons. Jackson had pre-arranged this with his client and had called ahead on their way to provide details of the vehicle they would be arriving in.

They were met by the general manager of the park who introduced himself to each of them with the deference due to owner's representatives. He would be personally conducting the tour, which he said would take two to three hours. The theme park had countless rides and attractions and covered a vast area. It was a nice change to be amongst such frivolity instead of the high tension of the past couple of days.

Chapter 14

Earlier that morning, Murray Jensen, Luna Smythe, Ping Xiaoyan and Yen Chow Yu met at Xiao's hotel in central Rome.

Xiao showed them into a private meeting room she had arranged. Jensen approved, expecting that some of their discussions might become heated.

'My Colombian clients were initially a little surprised at the involvement of the Sicilian mafia in the deal. I managed to convince them that the arrangements will result in a win for all parties. Their monies will be converted into a safe asset via a process that should not attract the scrutiny of the authorities. In turn, you will be paid the agreed fifteen percent fee, which you will share with the mafia as you see fit. I will receive the promised fee from my client at the successful conclusion of the transaction. A win all round.' Jensen thought he'd begin the discussion on common ground.

'What about the exclusivity of territory issue I raised in our call? This is a non-negotiable for my local contacts,' Xiao said, her eyes narrowing.

'No issues there,' Jensen responded confidently. He leaned back in his chair and clasped his hands behind his head before continuing. 'My Colombian friends are well aware of what is at stake here. They are keen to ensure a smooth conversion of their funds and do not wish in any way to inhibit that by starting a turf war.'

Jensen could see that Xiao had relaxed a little. Yu had not.

Jensen changed tack, leaning forward in his chair and speaking through clenched teeth. 'Now tell me about that fucker Tom Jackson. How long have you known of Jackson's involvement? Why didn't you inform me? Why do you have him under surveillance?' He was breathing heavily and making sweeping hand gestures. He couldn't help himself. He was so pissed off.

Yu rose from his chair and took an aggressive stance one pace behind Xiao. He was clearly a threat, although not the primary threat. Xiao had transformed. One moment she was listening respectfully to Jensen, and the next she was again the cobra poised to strike and inject her venom into his face. He now remembered who she reminded him of. It was Madeline Peel, the ruthless assassin known as the ghost. Peel was killed six months ago in London by Adrian Low. Low was the head of the Hong Kong-based syndicate up until his own death at the hands of a sniper, not long after he had expertly dispatched Peel. The presumption was that Peel had displeased him and was a loose end to be dealt with. It was a little-known fact that, prior to his elevation to the head of the syndicate, Low had been its most successful killing machine.

Xiao's startling metamorphosis caused Jensen to rethink his aggression. 'Let me back up a little. How about I let you explain in more detail exactly what is going on with Jackson.' Jensen could see that Xiao was pleased at his change in attitude.

'I told you I would explain more when we met,' Xiao began, signalling to Yu to resume his seat beside her. He did so, although he remained on the edge of his seat, leaning forward slightly so he could spring into action if the need arose. 'I became aware of Tom Jackson's involvement in the deal after our London lawyer informed me he was representing the seller. That was only a few days ago. There was no need for him to tell me prior to that. He let me know as soon as he became aware Jackson was coming to Rome to work on the deal. I intended to tell you at an appropriate time, and that is now.'

'I'm curious as to why you didn't tell me when we met in Portugal?' Jensen had managed to fully suppress his anger.

'You know why, Murray. That bastard has done real damage to both of us, and we *will* get even with him. Our syndicate has been dismembered thanks to Tom Jackson and Jason Jones. You lost your entire London operation and have spent the last six months in South America hiding out and rebuilding your network and reputation. I don't want our personal vendettas to get in the way of a great deal,' Xiao said forcefully.

'Then why are you having him tailed by the mafia's goons?' Jensen rubbed the back of his neck.

'Ah, good question. I was told by Matteo Ricci that his people are the best, and took him at his word. Assuming that to be the case, there will be no harm done in my knowing exactly where Jackson is at all times. I do not want him to leave Rome alive. My revenge is personal, although, like yours, it will need to wait until after the deal has been finalised and all the money is where it should be.'

'What do you mean by personal? Mine is bloody personal too, you know.' Jensen's voice was laced with sarcasm.

'He and Jones are responsible for the death of my father.' Xiao's direct stare lacked warmth.

Yu snapped his head to his right to observe Xiao with a questioning look in his eyes. She had everyone's full attention, and none dared speak.

'Adrian Low was my father.' Xiao let the words hang in the air before continuing. 'If it weren't for Tom fucking Jackson and Jason fucking Jones, he might still be alive. My father did take an unnecessary risk by becoming personally involved with the dodgy third-party banking intermediary in Cairo, but that should not have ended in his death. It's the primary reason I have fostered the new laundering arrangement with the mafia. The cloak of legitimacy when dealing with funds from Swiss bank accounts means there is very little risk of exposure.'

Yu's mouth had fallen open. 'I had no idea. I'm sorry, Xiao.'

'It was not widely known.' Xiao stared down at her hands before regaining her composure. 'In any event, now you might understand the extra imperative I have to ensure I know where Jackson is at all times. If I get a hint that the mafia's people are not up to it, I'll tell them to leave him alone for now, and instead monitor his comings and goings to and from his hotel.'

'I get it now.' Jensen offered his best impression of sympathy. 'I also agree we need to make sure Jackson is not tipped off to anything untoward.'

'I have a contact in Andrich Wiley, and she has advised that their partner, Lorenzo Bassutri, will be with Jackson at the Mondo Dei Sogni theme park this afternoon for a tour. We should definitely stay well away. I'll get a report on surveillance later in the day.' Xaio stood as if to conclude the meeting.

Jensen also stood. He was happy for the meeting to be over, and deliberately avoided promising to give Jackson a wide berth. He would regroup with Luna Smythe at their hotel to work out their next steps.

*

Jason Jones arrived on his flight from Australia shortly after midday. By the time he collected his luggage and made his way to the Colonna Palace Hotel, it was a little after two p.m. Tom had sent him an email while he was in-flight providing details of the day's scheduled events. After settling in to his room, Jason checked his watch and saw that by now Tom and Willow should be at the theme park. He messaged Jackson to let him know he had arrived, and asked if Tom thought he should join them at the park. Jackson's reply was that he and Willow had things under control and that they had not yet become aware of any credible threat. Jason responded that he would see them for dinner at the hotel.

Chapter 15

Tom looked up from his phone and leaned over to whisper to Willow as they began their tour of the theme park. 'That was Jason. He's arrived at our hotel here in Rome. He wanted to know if he should join us here. I told him you and I had things under control and that we'd catch up with him at the hotel for dinner later.'

'Good call,' Willow replied. 'We need him to get some rest after his long trip so that he is on his A-game in case his assistance is required.'

The general manager of the theme park had been there for almost ten years. His knowledge of the park and its history was extensive. He knew that Jackson's clients had owned the park for three years and pointed out each enhancement that had been made during that period. Tom was well aware of each new attraction and ride, as he had undertaken almost all of the associated legal work. It was always a thrill to see the finished product, and to hear and see the obvious joy of the patrons.

Tom's client had added a monster new rollercoaster ride, the highest and fastest in Europe. The sign adjacent to the ride advertised a one hour wait in the queue. Those in the queue were all in good spirits and chatting animatedly in anticipation of their impending adrenaline rush.

As they passed each ride, Lorenzo boasted how many times he and his two children had ridden on it, making good use of their season passes. Francesca was also a regular visitor to the park, and she shared Lorenzo's enthusiasm. She was constantly throwing her head back and laughing loudly at the sky.

They moved on to an open section of the park, which contained countless indoor and outdoor food areas. Huge shade trees were strategically positioned around the outdoor seating areas. These included iconic umbrella pine trees, a variety of olive trees and a massive evergreen cork oak in the centre.

'I need to visit the toilet. I won't be long. It's just on the rise behind those buildings over there.' Francesca was pointing straight ahead. 'Any other takers?' There were none.

'We might just grab a bottle of water for each of us. We'll wait for you here, Francesca,' Tom said thoughtfully.

*

Francesca walked in the direction of the toilets, looking over her shoulder with a look of consternation on her face. She was wondering why Willow Douglas had joined Tom in Rome. Willow was so attractive, and tall. Francesca could not tell with any certainty if there was any kind of relationship between the two. Her instincts told her there was. She was mulling this over as she left the bathroom when she noticed a suspicious-looking pair. One had binoculars and they were both staring in the direction of her party, speaking quietly and rapidly to each other.

'Mi scusi, excuse me, please.' The pair was partially blocking Francesca's path back to her colleagues.

The Lombordo siblings turned as one, and each registered shock at the prospect of having again been spotted in their surveillance activities. They had no doubt recognised Francesca as a member of the group they were keeping tabs on.

In a well-practiced movement, Dante Lombordo grabbed Francesca around the throat. He roughly placed his other hand over her mouth to stifle her scream. Francesca struggled and tried to escape. Her eyes widened in fear as she saw Caterina Lombordo calmly remove a switch blade from her pocket and press the button on the side, causing the razor-sharp blade to spring out. Without any apparent thought, Caterina plunged the blade into the side of Francesca's neck.

As Francesca's life blood drained quickly from her, she heard the Lombordo siblings agree that they'd had no choice. They had been discovered. They took Francesca's purse and mobile phone to make it look like a robbery.

*

'I wonder what's taking Francesca so long? I need to use the convenience myself now. I'll go and check on her.' Willow headed towards the toilets. She had not taken more than a few paces before they all heard a blood-curdling scream from the direction she was headed. In an instant, Tom was on his feet, and they were both jogging in the direction of the scream. Willow had drawn her gun, and Tom had his Swiss army knife at the ready.

The site that met them was completely unexpected. Francesca was lying on her back in a pool of blood, her unseeing eyes staring into nothing. Her long shiny brown hair was matted with a dark sticky substance Jackson knew to be her own blood.

'What the fuck happened here!' Tom was on high alert looking in all directions.

Lorrenzo had arrived and immediately doubled over and vomited. Tom was also in shock although able to process it differently because of his training, and his recent experiences with death. He was having trouble communicating with bystanders, and asked Lorenzo if he could please assist. He could hear many of them calling out 'Dial 113', which was the number for the polizia.

Willow was sprinting in the direction in which many of the bystanders were pointing. Tom stood to follow her path. There were two persons in the distance getting into a worker's vehicle to make good their escape. A man and a woman. She was wearing a turquoise sweater, and he had on a light green windcheater.

Willow returned to the group shortly afterwards, breathing heavily. 'Motherfuckers got away. What on earth could they have been thinking? It defies belief that they would stoop this low. What could they possibly gain from Francesca's death?' Willow's emotions were bubbling over.

Tom could hear the sirens approaching as he put a reassuring hand on Willow's shoulder. 'A warning maybe? But I wonder what for? We might now need to carefully revisit every aspect of this deal.'

Bassutri had joined them, and was shaking his head from side to side. 'I can't believe what I'm seeing. Such a waste, and for what!' He tore his eyes away from the gruesome scene and faced Tom and Willow, doing his best to put on a brave face. 'You're right, we do need to refocus. I did hear my personal assistant telling someone on the phone late yesterday that we would be touring the theme park this afternoon. I didn't think anything of it at the time. Now that this abhorrent act has occurred, I'll speak with her pronto to ask her about it.'

Emergency personnel were quickly on the scene. With Lorenzo's assistance, the police quickly established the details of what had occurred, and who had been with Francesca immediately before she met her brutal end. They made a note of the personal details for all three and conducted brief interviews as Francesca's body was removed. Having established that Francesca's purse and mobile phone had been taken, the police formed the preliminary view that Francesca was the unfortunate victim of a botched robbery.

Tom and Willow independently came to the view that it was best at this stage not to let the police know they had previously seen the pair likely responsible for the killing. To do otherwise would tie them both up for some time with interviews.

'We need to be free agents to have a look into this ourselves,' Tom spoke quietly to Willow after the police left. 'Imagine having to explain the events of the last couple of years, which may or may not be connected with this.'

They had been close to completing their tour of the theme park when the unbelievable events had unfolded. It was early evening before the police completed their investigations and they were allowed to leave.

'I'm so sorry, Lorenzo. This must be very difficult for you.' Tom gently patted Lorenzo's back.

'Grazie, Tom. I am still in shock. I can't imagine who would kill someone as innocent and lovely as Francesca, simply to steal her purse and cell phone.' Lorenzo'a posture was stooped, and he looked exhausted.

'Why don't we have a rest day tomorrow, Lorenzo, and regroup on Monday morning in your office. Can your driver drop us off at our hotel?' Jackson continued.

'Of course.' Lorenzo suddenly stood more upright as if to shake off his grief. 'I almost forgot to mention something to you.' Jackson nodded, encouraging Lorenzo to continue. 'While the police were investigating, I called my personal assistant. She confirmed that she had been speaking with a lady with a Chinese accent when I overheard her on the phone yesterday. I pressed her and she admitted there had been one other conversation the day before in which she divulged that a second Terms Sheet was in play. Needless to say, she has been summarily dismissed.'

Jackson looked at Willow, who was also frowning. 'Did she say who the person was and why she was passing on information?'

'Not exactly. Just that she had received an envelope with five thousand euros in cash immediately before the first phone call. The information was given in exchange for the cash, with more promised. Unfortunately, her mother has been quite ill lately and I was aware that the unpaid medical bills had been mounting. I had been speaking with my partners about providing temporary financial assistance, although I hadn't yet had the opportunity to talk to her about it. Water under the bridge now.'

'We have a lot to process.' Tom avoided eye contact with the others as they made their way to the law firm's limousine.

Chapter 16

Dante and Caterina Lombordo called their boss, Matteo Ricci, after making good their escape from the theme park.

'There's been a complication boss.' The self-loathing was evident in Dante's voice.

'What have you two idiots done now?' Matteo Ricci yelled into the phone.

The Lombordo siblings exchanged a nervous look before Dante continued. 'We tracked Jackson and his party to the Mondo Dei Sogni theme park, as instructed. But we were spotted by the junior lawyer from Andrich Wiley as she was coming out of the bathroom. Our instincts kicked in and we reacted.'

Ricci was scrolling through news stories on his tablet as they spoke. He couldn't believe what he was reading. 'You mean you panicked and slit her throat, you fucking morons!' He let out a guttural raw at their sheer idiocy.

'We had no choice, boss. She would have exposed us. We took her purse and cell phone to make it look like a robbery,' Caterina pleaded.

'You have exposed yourselves. The news flash I'm looking at says a man and a woman with similar features were observed running from the scene.' Ricci's voice was calmer now. He knew exactly how to proceed. 'Do you know where our safe house is in Ostia just south of the Fiumicino International Airport?'

'Yes, boss,' the Lombordo siblings chimed together.

'Head there now and await instructions.' Ricci ended the call without further discussion. He was livid as he dialled the cell phone of the mafia's chief enforcer in Rome.

'Ciao, boss.' The enforcer answered on the first ring.

'We have a situation that needs to be contained immediately. Head to our safe house in Ostia. Dante and Caterina Lombordo are on their way there now. They have fucked up for the last time. Go there and eliminate both of them and dispose of their bodies so that no trace of them remains.' Ricci knew that the threatening tone in his voice would leave no doubt in the mind of his enforcer that he was to follow the instructions to the letter.

'It will be done.'

Matteo Ricci ended the call and focused on what he would tell that scary bitch, Ping Xiaoyan. He knew he did not have the luxury of time. The story would be all over the news, and he wanted Xiao to hear it from him.

'Xiao, it's Matteo Ricci. Our surveillance did not go well today.' *Rip the band-aid off*, he told himself.

'Explain.' Xiao responded through clenched teeth, while activating the speaker mode on her phone so that Yu could hear.

'My operatives were discovered by the young lawyer from Andrich Wiley who had accompanied Jackson to the theme park. They panicked and killed her, taking her valuables to make it look like a robbery gone bad.'

'You're joking, of course. You said your operatives were the best at surveillance.'

Ricci could almost feel her anger through the phone.

'They were good but have let me down on a couple of occasions now.' He knew he'd made an error as soon as he uttered the words.

Xiao responded with cat-like instincts. 'What else have they done?'

Too late now. 'They think they were spotted by Tom Jackson on at least one occasion, and possibly two,' Ricci confessed.

'You fucking moron! You have placed our entire arrangements in jeopardy. The very last thing we need is for Jackson's suspicions to be aroused, for any reason!' Xiao was as furious as he was.

Unaccustomed to being berated by anyone, and in particular a woman, Matteo Ricci pushed back. 'Then I think you may need to consider the implications of your own decision to have Jackson tailed. Why did you, anyway?'

Xiao did not respond directly to his question. 'Careful, Matteo. Remember who you are dealing with.'

For some inexplicable reason, Ricci felt his blood run cold. He could visualise the anger in those eyes that radiated death.

'I apologise unreservedly, Signora Xiao. With your permission I will cease any further surveillance. I have also ensured that the two members of the surveillance team will never be heard from again.' Ricci was holding his breath.

'Apology accepted. This time. Cease surveillance. It's very lucky for you that you have eliminated the problem.' Xiao ended the call.

*

Xiao put her cell phone down on the table and turned to Yu, fuming. 'We need some damage control. I'll call Jensen now and fill him in on the details.'

'Murray, I have received my report on today's surveillance.' Xiao proceeded to explain all that the mafia boss had told her.

'You're shitting me.' Jensen sounded exasperated.

'Surveillance has ceased, and plans are in place to dispatch the incompetent pair in question this evening. I've looked at the breaking news stories and the initial view of the authorities is that it was a botched robbery. Our biggest problem is that Tom Jackson is now aware he is under surveillance, and apparently has been for a couple of days.'

Xiao knew that Jensen had not committed to staying away from Jackson and decided to press the point. 'I suggest we forget how we got here and deal with what's next. Can I have your assurance that you will back off any intended surveillance of your own on Jackson? We need to let things settle so that we can all focus on the deal.'

'I have brought in further resources that I agree to put on ice, for now. Like you, I will not let Tom Jackson leave Rome alive.'

'Thank you, and I am sorry we find ourselves in this position.' Contrition, even feigned contrition, was not usually her style. She winked at Yu, who was observing her thoughtfully, almost as if he thought she might be unwell. 'Jackson might be minded to kick over a few rocks to see if he can discover anything untoward. I am sure he will not find anything, so long as we both keep a low profile from here.'

'You're right. Let's back off Jackson completely and let the lawyers do their thing. You focus on the availability of the funding. I'll deploy my assets near Jackson's hotel on a rotational basis, with a watching brief only. I'll tell them avoiding detection is paramount. The London lawyer will no doubt let you know if any change in Jackson's location is likely. I see no need to unnecessarily alarm my Colombian drug cartel by letting them know anything about this.'

'Agree, and in particular not bothering the cartel with the detail of today's events.' Xiao felt some of the tension leave her shoulders.

Unbeknownst to both Ping Xiaoyan and Murray Jensen, the Colombian drug cartel was already aware of the unwanted attention. With €200 million of their own funds at risk, they had already established a channel of communication with Matteo Ricci's immediate superior within the Sicilian mafia.

Within the hour, Jensen had received a call from his key contact within the drug cartel, its head of security. He advised they were aware of exactly what was happening in Rome, and cautioned against any further lapses of judgement that might in any way put their funds at risk.

*

Tom and Willow were relieved to be back at their hotel. Tom had phoned Jason Jones during their limousine ride, and Jones met them in the reception area.

'So good to see you, Jonesy.' Tom and Jason embraced in a man hug, much to Willow's amusement.

'Hey, you two. Save some for me.'

Jones beamed as he turned to Willow and embraced her as a true friend. They had been through a lot together in London the prior year.

'I've booked a private booth in a nearby restaurant that the hotel's concierge recommended to me.' Jones looked well rested.

'Good idea. We have plenty to tell you.' Tom headed out the front door in the direction Jones had indicated. 'I sure could use a grande drink.'

Jones raised his eyebrows and shrugged his shoulders. Willow pressed her lips together, nodded and turned to follow Tom out the door.

Chapter 17

DAY 7 (Sunday)

Tom, Willow and Jason met for breakfast on the rooftop of the Colonna Palace Hotel. Jones had arrived first, and was enjoying the historic vista when Tom and Willow got there.

'Buongiorno. Unbelievable outlook.' Jackson and Willow nodded their agreement while taking their seats at the table as Jones continued. 'I've been thinking about the events of the last few days, mate. Surveillance, bribery and murder? I know I shouldn't be surprised, but I am.'

'We need to piece everything together to establish any common links. Until we do that, we will not know what's at stake or how to keep ourselves safe.' Willow was looking intently at both of them.

Jackson signalled the waiter to bring each of them a freshly made barista coffee. He functioned better in the morning after caffeine. 'I agree. None of us believes in coincidence, so this must all be connected in some way.' Jackson leaned forward on his elbows and rested his chin on steepled hands. 'Our experience tells us that these kinds of threats are usually associated with a broader purpose. Let's think about this for a moment. I'm being followed and those responsible are committed enough to their cause to resort to murder to avoid detection. Ironically, the outcome of their actions has been to attract attention to themselves. There is also someone willing to pay large sums of cash to procure information about the deal I'm here to work on.'

'It's almost like amateur hour. I wonder if...' Jones ran his hand over the top of his army-style buzz haircut, his voice trailing off as he spoke.

'What?' Tom and Willow said together.

'Well, I've been thinking.' Jones had Tom and Willow's full attention. 'None of your searches has identified any issue with either the buyer or their likely source of funds.' Jackson nodded. 'So why the need for amateurish surveillance and information gathering?' Jones answered his own question. 'There's definitely something going on here. Maybe the events are not connected. Let's look at the events in isolation. Those most likely to gain from inside knowledge of the deal are either part of the process that is running, or part of the competing backup deal, which is being progressed in parallel. Commercial espionage is not in itself unusual, and advance knowledge of events can be valuable enough to pay decent sums of cash for. We have to wonder about the lady with the Chinese accent, mate.'

'I'm with you so far.' Tom was happy for Jones to fully explore his thought processes.

'Then there's the surveillance. What the hell could be gained by someone knowing your every move, and why allocate inexperienced drongos to the task? It doesn't make any sense, unless...'

'What?' Tom and Willow said together again, their growing frustration evident.

'The events are connected. I think we're dealing with illicit funds again, Tom, and whoever is involved knows that you're a threat to them. That means they're aware of the significance of your involvement, either from personal experience or from reading about your exploits. The low-level surveillance would suggest that someone has a personal interest in your whereabouts and is trying to be less obtrusive to whomever they are working for or with, by deploying less-significant assets to the task. As you say, it's ironic that this approach has had exactly the opposite outcome. Not only are we having these conversations, but I'm sure others are too. My guess is they'll back off for now, and leave the apparently legitimate process to play out.'

'Any suggestions?' Jackson queried.

'If I'm right then we're dealing with real threats here. I suggest we deploy some countermeasures of our own. Since you and Willow have already been seen together on many occasions, you should continue to do everything together. I expect that my presence has not yet been detected. I'll follow your movements at a distance to see if you still have a tail. I'll be able to get to you quickly if there is anything either of you need help with. Maybe you can also ask Bassutri to ramp up his own anti-bribery and corruption enquiries about the declared source of funds.'

'So effectively, I'll be the bait to draw out any criminal low-lifes.' Tom was experiencing a mixture of apprehension and excitement. He knew there were those associated with the criminal organisations that he had helped take down last year who were still at large. If Jason was correct in his thinking on this, then the unfolding dangerous situation might present an opportunity to complete the tasks from last year. 'Should we get our friends at INTERPOL involved in this?'

'Not yet, mate. Let's give it a day or two to see what develops, and exercise extreme bloody care in the meantime.'

'Roger that,' Willow said.

Jackson could see that both of his companions were in their element. He had been here before and knew what to expect. It wasn't his day job, however, and he reminded himself that a cautious approach would be prudent. 'Okay, fine. Let's enjoy some of Rome today, and maybe not wander too far. See what we flush out.' Tom leaned back in his seat to enjoy his coffee.

*

What none of them knew was that Murray Jensen's assets were already on site. They were not amateurs. One of the pair had taken a position at ground level from where he could observe the hotel entrance. The other was on a nearby roof and had already taken a long-range photo of the three of them as they enjoyed their rooftop breakfast.

'What the fuck,' Jensen exclaimed as he saw the grainy photo appear on his phone. He leaned over to Luna Smythe and showed her the photo. 'That's definitely Tom Jackson, and the woman looks familiar. I may have seen her before in London. It's a little more difficult to make out the facial features of the third person, but I'd know that physique and buzz-cut anywhere. That's the one and only Jason Jones.' Jensen had a broad grin on his face as he looked up at Luna. She frowned and tilted her head questioningly to the side. 'You know what this means, Luna?' He stood and grabbed her by the shoulders and was about to give her a hug. He stopped himself and stood back a pace. 'I have both of them in my sights now.'

'But we've agreed with Xiao not to do anything other than to maintain covert surveillance for now. The cartel has also warned us in no uncertain terms,' Smythe reminded him.

Jensen shushed her by putting a finger to her lips.

Chapter 18

Murray Jensen dialled Ping Xiaoyan's cell phone. 'Xiao, it's Jensen.'

'Yes, I see that. I thought we agreed to keep a low profile for a while.' Xiao's tone was sharp.

'That big bastard Jason Jones is in town.'

'Are you certain?'

'Have a look at the photo I'm sending you now.'

'You're right. We now have both of those meddling bastards in our sights.'

'My thoughts exactly. Jones got away from me once. I'm not prepared to take the chance that he'll do the same again. They're both here now.' Jensen did not wish to tell Xiao that he had been warned off personal vendettas by the head of security for the Colombian drug cartel. Maybe he could persuade Xiao to do the dirty work and he could maintain a level of deniability.

'As tempting as it is, we can't do anything just yet. We need Jackson to complete the deal first.' Jensen was unaware that Xiao had also been warned by senior members of the Sicilian mafia to step back and allow the deal to proceed.

'How about we acquire Jones and use his capture as leverage against Jackson.' Jensen was restless, holding his breath.

'It's not worth the risk. That tactic didn't work for you in London last year, and you didn't then have the added disadvantage of powerful allies such as the Sicilian mafia and the Colombian drug cartel breathing down your neck and watching every move. They will only be our allies for as long as we keep to the script. Patience, Jensen, patience.'

'Maybe you're right. Let's chat again in a couple of days.' Jensen could see that if he was going to do anything, it would need to be on his own.

'Very wise. I'll call you on Tuesday, unless something comes up beforehand. In the meantime, it might be best to ask your assets to stand down.' Xiao ended the call abruptly.

Jensen looked at the phone, then at Luna Smythe. 'Fucking pussy. She's not prepared to do anything, even though we might not get such an opportunity again.'

Luna Smythe remained silent, as she bloody well should, thought Jensen. He chose to ignore her obvious concern.

Jensen activated his secure comms that were connected to his assets who had staked out Jackson's hotel. 'Jensen here. Call in.'

'Check one.' Came the first response, quickly followed by, 'Check two.'

'Do you have eyes on?'

'This is one. I'm on a nearby roof from where I took the photo I sent through. I have eyes on the party of three. I've shared the photo with two.'

'This is two. I'm in position outside the hotel to follow the party at a distance, as instructed.'

'Change of plan.' Jensen winked at Luna, who was gently shaking her head from side to side, her eyes widening. 'Do you have transport?' Jensen continued.

'This is two. I have a van nearby. What's your wish, boss.'

'The one with the buzz-cut is Jason Jones. The other male is Tom Jackson, and I'm not sure who the woman is. Jones and Jackson are highly trained in some form of martial arts, and if the woman is who I think she is, she too will have training. Treat all three as extremely dangerous, even if unarmed.'

'Copy that.' Jensen's operatives responded almost at the same time.

'Acquire Jones, unharmed if possible. If not, maimed is fine, just don't kill him. We need him alive. Don't hurt Jackson, but kill the bitch if she gets in the way. Jackson must be allowed to escape unharmed.'

'This is two. Preferred timing?'

'Imperative that Jones is acquired today. Secure him well and take him to the apartment you're staying in. Let me know when you get there, and I'll be there shortly after.'

'Copy that,' Two responded.

Jensen continued after a brief pause. 'On second thoughts, I'll join you in the van. I can't wait to see the expression on Jones' fucking face when he's recaptured. I'll be at your site in fifteen minutes.'

Smythe again remained silent. Jensen could see the distinct look of disapproval in her eyes. He shrugged his shoulders and headed out for Jackson's hotel, signalling for Smythe to stay put.

*

'Okay, where to?' Jackson stood from the breakfast table on the rooftop of their hotel, shrugging into his light jacket.

'I'm sure you two have been here plenty of times, so I think I should choose.' Willow had a sparkle in her eye. 'While I think of it, here Jason, take this.' She handed Jones her spare hand gun. 'Do you still have your boy scout knife, Tom?' Jackson nodded with a grin, patting his jacket pocket. 'Good then, let's go.'

'Can I ask where? It'll make it a little easier to keep tabs on you from a distance if I have some idea of where you're headed,' Jones responded without emotion.

Tom reminded himself why these two professionals were so calm in situations like this. They both had extensive training and combat zone experience.

'I knew you'd ask.' Willow smiled. 'I'd like to spend most of the day on foot, subject of course to there being no outside interference. I'm thinking the Pantheon, then Piazza Navona for a second coffee, some music and people watching. After that we can walk across the River Tiber to Castel Sant'Angelo, the second-century cylindrical castle and museum that features in Dan Brown's Da Vinci Code. Then on to St Peter's Basilica for a gander at the world's largest basilica of Christianity. I've heard that it's possible to visit the Papal tombs downstairs, which I'd absolutely love to do. I'll let one of you two decide on the venue for a late lunch or early dinner, so keep an eye out on the way.'

'Sounds great.' Jackson had difficulty hiding his enthusiasm.

'Okay. They're all busy places, and it is Sunday. I might need to stay a little closer. That'll mean I'll need both of your assistance to spot any bad guys.' Jones handed each of them a small ear piece for secure communication. 'Let's test them now. The range is five hundred metres. If we get separated beyond range, let's use the short-form emergency cell phone texts we agreed in London.'

'Roger that,' Tom said, causing the other two to laugh out loud.

Chapter 19

Murray Jensen arrived at the Colonna Palace Hotel and linked up with his two operatives just in time to see Jackson and Willow leave the hotel.

'They're on foot, probably sightseeing. One, you and I will follow on foot at a distance. Two, you make sure you're close by when I signal it's time for the extraction.' Jensen was scanning the area for Jones. 'I don't see Jones anywhere yet. One, you go ahead now and tail Jackson and the tall blonde, and I'll hang back a little to see if I can spot Jones. He may be planning to join them later, or may himself have stayed back intentionally to provide cover.'

'At your nine o'clock,' Two said quietly after a short time.

Jensen could see that Jones had left via the hotel's side exit and was headed in the same direction as Jackson and the woman. 'One, be advised. Jones is headed in your direction as cover for Jackson. Stand aside carefully if you can, and I'll join you. Resume surveillance after Jones passes you, whether I've caught up or not.' He left the other operative, signalling him to return and collect the van.

*

'Tom, Willow, do you copy?' They each tapped their earpiece once to acknowledge. 'I may have spotted a bogey on your tail. Wait one. No, maybe not. He's veered off your path. He had that look about him and moved like a professional. Keep an eye out for him. He's around six foot tall with a brown jacket and a black baseball cap over shoulder-length black hair.' Tom and Willow tapped their earpieces once without breaking stride or looking around.

Tom cast a sideways glance at Willow, and she winked and walked on. 'I trust Jason and you should too, Tom. We both have guns and, as you put it earlier, all three of us know exactly how to make use of our body parts as weapons.' That made Tom smile, even though it did not lower his level of apprehension.

Tom felt like a tour guide as they made their way to the Pantheon and then on to Piazza Navona. Willow spotted a pair about to leave a table for two facing the Piazza, and swooped on it as soon as they had vacated their seats. They ordered coffee while they took in the sights and sounds of the famous piazza. At the same time, they were both scanning the area for the man in the brown jacket and black cap Jones had spotted.

Jones had built a global reputation for his business based on both skills and innate instincts. He had expertly doubled back after Tom and Willow left the Pantheon. While waiting patiently in the shadows, he again identified the tail. 'I think your bogey is back. I'll keep an eye on him.'

'Copy,' Willow said quietly, looking at Tom.

*

Jensen thought better of joining his operative. He had too much respect for Jones and had waited before heading in the direction taken by Jackson and his companion. After Jackson had left the Pantheon, followed by operative one, Jensen had spotted Jones waiting in the shadows before taking up his own pursuit.

'One, this is control. Jones has doubled back and is on your six. Keep moving. I've got you covered.'

'Roger that. They've just taken a table in a café in Piazza Navona,' One responded.

'Two, do you read.' Jensen had switched radio frequency as previously arranged with his driver.

'Copy,' Two replied.

'Pick me up here in a couple of minutes.' Jensen dropped a pin on a map on a street between the Pantheon and Piazza Navona.

Jensen joined his operative in the van, and they merged with the traffic heading towards his prey. 'Pull over there and activate your hazard lights.' Jensen was pointing to a loading zone.

Jensen resumed shared comms. 'One, let me know when they leave the café.'

'On the move again now, boss. They're heading towards the northern end of the piazza. My guess is they plan to cross the River Tiber via Ponte Umberto 1, heading towards St Peter's Basilica and other nearby tourist sites.'

'Perfect. I'm with two in the van, heading in your direction. Assuming you're right, let me know when you're nearly over the bridge. We should be able to trap Jones on the bridge between us, and capture him.'

'In position now, boss.'

'On our way.'

As Jensen's van approached the bridge, he heard an engine roar to their left. He looked in the direction of the sound, just in time to see a black suburban careening towards them. The impact was violent and loud. The crunch of metal on metal was not something Jensen would forget in a hurry.

Time slowed for Jensen. He looked over at his driver and saw that he was seriously injured, bleeding heavily from a head wound. Through the driver's window he could see the relatively undamaged black suburban backing away when two men leapt out. The two strangers ran to his side of the van and slid open the undamaged door. To onlookers, the strangers would be checking to see if those in the damaged vehicle were okay. They pushed their way into the van, even before Jensen had regained his senses and unbuckled his seatbelt, and expertly snapped the driver's neck.

Jensen's last thought as he felt the strong hands grasp both sides of his neck was that he should have listened to Xiao.

The intruders returned to the black suburban, which left as quickly as it had arrived.

First on the scene was Jensen's remaining operative. He quickly took in the scene. The departing black suburban had no plates. The odd angle of the heads of both his boss and fellow operative left no room for mistaking their fate. He turned and melted into the growing crowd of tourists. Whistles were blowing and sirens blaring as emergency personnel approached.

*

Jones heard the sickening crunch of metal behind him at the entrance to the bridge he was crossing. He turned and like most had remained stationary, assessing the situation. His quarry in the brown jacket and black cap rushed past him towards the mangled van. Jones saw him look quickly in the van and then turn and mingle with the crowd.

'Tom, Willow. Did you hear that?'

'Sure did. Are you okay?' Jackson was first to respond.

'Affirmative. Stay where you are, and I'll check it out. It must be connected with your bogey who immediately jogged back to take in the crash site. He took one look inside, looked around like a scared rabbit, and then quickly faded into the crowd.'

Jones walked briskly across the bridge to join the throngs of people. He couldn't tell if most of them were converging on the crash site to offer assistance, or simply gawk. Probably both.

He realised he had to move quickly. He could see uniformed officers approaching from every direction. They would shortly take control and cordon off the area. He pushed his way to the front of the growing mass of onlookers but was not prepared for what he saw. Both the driver and his passenger looked to have broken their necks in the accident. The driver had suffered extensive head injuries. The passenger, however, did not look to have suffered trauma from the crash itself. He was nevertheless just as dead. Jones could see the slight telltale signs on both sides of the passenger's neck. As soon as he looked at the passenger's face, he realised he had to leave.

'Tom, Willow. I'm heading your way.' Jones caught up with them both and directed them into a nearby park area that had emptied of tourists who had all rushed to look at the scene on the bridge. 'You won't fucking believe this. After I heard the crash, I turned to see a black suburban reversing away from the seriously damaged van. Two heavy-looking guys hopped out and looked into the van. I thought they might have been checking on the occupants, but I now think they were there to finish the job and kill the driver and his passenger.'

'What makes you say that?' Willow was on full alert.

'The driver was messed up from the crash, and clearly deceased. Broken neck. His passenger wasn't banged up at all from the crash, but his neck was also broken. It looks like they both had their necks snapped after the accident.'

'Holy shit. So if those in the van were connected to our tail, who were the thugs in the black suburban?' Tom was as alert as his two colleagues.

'That's the sixty-four-dollar question, Tom,' Jones continued. 'And here's the kicker. The deceased passenger was none other than Murray Jensen.'

'You're certain?' Tom's mouth had fallen open.

'Affirmative. Let's hightail it out of here and regroup at the hotel. Heads on a swivel on the way back.'

The three of them moved at a fast walk towards the next bridge crossing the river, headed in the direction of their hotel. They did not wish to attract any attention.

Chapter 20

DAY 8 (Monday)

Matteo Ricci called Ping Xiaoyan. 'Xiao, it's Matteo.'

'It's early. What could you possibly want at this hour?' Xiao had been awake for a while, undertaking her extensive daily exercise routine.

'When was the last time you spoke to Murray Jensen?'

'Yesterday morning. Why?'

'Did the two of you discuss further surveillance of Jackson and his group?'

'We did, and agreed that we'd back off for now and allow the deal to proceed, particularly after the heat that your people caused on Saturday.' Xiao knew that she had ordered the surveillance of Jackson. It would not have been a problem if those morons hadn't slit that woman's throat. She reminded herself that she had been entitled to assume a level of competence from the mafia's people.

'Well, Jensen obviously didn't listen to you. He was observed yesterday shadowing Jackson and his group. I am told he was about to apprehend Jackson's colleague, Jones I think you said his name was. Once his intentions became clear, he was stopped.'

'Stopped? How, and by who?'

'I can't tell you who, although I can tell you that no one in Jackson's party was involved in any way. Murray Jensen was killed in the process, along with the driver of his vehicle. Another connection was seen running off into the crowd, and he has not been located.'

'So you're telling me Murray Jensen and one of his operatives are dead?' Xiao could not believe what she was hearing.

'Si.'

'Was the driver of the van male or female?'

'Male, why?'

'It's not your concern. Fuck! We may now be compromised beyond redemption.' Xiao was thinking quickly. She had put her phone on speaker mode shortly after the conversation had commenced and opened the door that linked her room with Yen Chow Yu's. Yu had joined her and heard most of the conversation.

'Si, and my grande capo, the big boss, is none too happy. We warned you, Xiao.' Xiao could hear in Ricci's voice that he was likely under pressure from his superiors.

'And I heeded that warning and told Jensen to also back off. He said he would. I need to think about this. I'll get back to you.' Xiao ended the call, and turned to Yu.

'We need to head straight to Jensen's hotel now and secure Luna Smythe.' Xiao was already headed for the door.

'I need to grab a couple of things from my room. I'll meet you in reception.' Yu was also on the move.

*

Luna Smythe was concerned that she had not heard from Murray Jensen since he rushed out the door shortly after breakfast yesterday, intent on capturing Jason Jones. She knew better than to interrupt Jensen while on an operation. He had not made contact overnight, and she had tried to reach him on a number of occasions that morning without success.

Luna was contemplating what to do next when there was a knock at her door.

'Who's there?' Smythe called out, her lips beginning to tremble. She was out of her depth, again. There was no peep hole in the door for her to see who was on the other side.

'It's Xiao. I need to speak with you urgently, Luna.'

Luna recognised Xiao's voice. 'Who's with you?'

'Yen Chow Yu is with me.'

'Where's Murray?'

'That's what I need to discuss with you.'

Luna didn't trust Xiao or Yu, but had little choice. She unbolted the door, leaving the security chain attached, and peered nervously through the opening.

Xiao and Yu had both stepped back from the door and adopted a non-threatening stance. Both were holding their empty hands in front of them, with their palms facing upwards.

'We need to talk to you, Luna, about your personal safety.'

Smythe told herself again that she did not have a choice. She unlatched the security chain and let them in.

'Thank you. May we take a seat?'

'Right over there.' Luna pointed. 'Where's Murray, and why are you here?'

'Both good questions.' Xiao leant forward on her seat and drew her eyebrows together. 'I'm sorry to tell you that Murray was killed yesterday in his attempts to capture Jason Jones.'

'What! Killed! You're kidding!' Luna's eyes were bulging, and she was speechless.

'I warned him not to. He said he agreed with my reasoning and told me he would stand down. It was the best way to allow the money laundering transaction to continue. I didn't tell him that the upper echelons of the mafia had warned me to stand down. I didn't think I needed to.'

'So you think the mafia killed Murray?' Luna was still coming to terms with what she was hearing.

'I don't think so. They would have taken the credit if it were them. No, I think it may have been Murray's connections in the Colombian drug cartel. My guess is they've already established communication channels with the mafia and know exactly what's been going on.'

'That fits.' Smythe crumpled back into her chair. 'Murray received a call from the head of security for the cartel on Saturday afternoon, not long after that woman was killed at the theme park. He said they were aware of exactly what had been happening in Rome and that Murray was to ensure there were no further lapses of judgement that might put their funds at risk.'

'Hmm. Murray didn't mention that,' Xiao began. 'It all makes sense now. It must have been the cartel who took him out.'

'So what now?' Until now, Yu had been listening intently.

'The problem we have is that we have been severely compromised.' Xiao sat back in her chair and folded her arms. 'It's hard to imagine that Tom Jackson is not on high alert after what happened over the weekend. He and Jones will keep digging now until they uncover the truth. The pendulum has swung from the presumption of a legitimate deal to exactly the opposite. Curse you and your impatience, Murray Jensen.'

'We have to assume then that the transaction to launder the cartel's funds by way of the purchase of the theme park will not now proceed.' Luna was coming out of shock and starting to think more clearly now. 'If that's true, then we are all at risk of retribution.'

'I agree. We need to relocate somewhere more secure.' Xiao stood and was beginning to pace back and forth. 'I will stay in touch with the London lawyer and my contact in the mafia in case there is any prospect of the deal proceeding. If it does fall apart then there will only be one thing left for me.'

'Revenge?' Yu was also now standing, moving lightly from one foot to the other.

'Exactly. Jackson and Jones were not only responsible for the death of my father, Adrian Low, but also for my older sister.'

'I didn't know you had a sister.' Yu had stopped moving and was looking intently at Xiao.

'Madeline Peel,' Xiao said quietly, staring at the floor.

'The ghost was your sister?' Yu was regarding Xiao with wide eyes and a new level of respect.

'She was. I understand why my father felt he had to kill her, but I will never forgive him for that.' Even so, Xiao would still avenge his death.

Luna knew Madeline Peel had been the most feared assassin for the Hong Kong-based criminal syndicate. Jensen had been right all along in thinking he saw a connection between Xiao and Peel. Adrian Low's killing of Peel in London six months ago took on a whole new meaning. 'So we're all fucked, thanks to Tom Jackson and Jason Jones. Do you have room for a tech expert on your team, Xiao?'

'Absolutely. Pack your things and let's get out of here.'

Chapter 21

Jackson, Willow and Jones met again for breakfast at the rooftop garden of their hotel. They had spent some time on Sunday afternoon dissecting the alarming events of the weekend, before deciding to order takeaway pizza and beer. Having determined that there was no known immediate threat to them in their hotel, they had all turned in for an early night, agreeing to strategise over breakfast.

'I ordered fresh coffee for all of us on the way in,' Tom began the conversation, as he joined Willow and Jason who were already seated at the table. Jason smiled, and Willow mouthed the words thank you. 'Looks like none of us slept much last night.'

'Correctamundo.' Jones was channelling 'The Fonz', an Italian American actor in the popular 1970s television series *Happy Days*. It brought a smile to Willow's tired visage, and that made Tom smile.

'I'll call Lorenzo Bassutri this morning to see how he's coping after Francesca's murder on Saturday.' Tom was sipping his cappuccino, which had arrived surprisingly quickly. 'He may not even be at work. If he is, I'll ask him to dig deeper with his anti-bribery and corruption enquiries. I haven't yet seen the results of the buyer's London lawyer's enquiries in this respect. I'll chase them up this morning.'

Jones perked up a little. 'I think it's time to bring INTERPOL into the loop. I'll make contact with both Inspector Lachlan Darwin in Aus and Inspector Wilfred Mason in London. They'll be interested to know that Murray Jensen was not only back on the scene, but is now deceased. They can liaise with Italian authorities, who I see are reporting simply that two foreigners suffered unfortunate fatal injuries in a hit and run car crash in central Rome yesterday afternoon.'

'Good idea.' Tom was nodding his head, which was becoming clearer with each sip of coffee. 'Maybe also mention the woman with the Chinese accent. I could be completely wrong here, but if Jensen was involved, then the resurrection of the Hong Kong-based syndicate might be as well. Willow, you might recall that two of the syndicate members were never captured.' As soon as he'd said it, Tom knew that the explanation to Willow was not necessary. She smiled as he continued. 'It might also be worth getting Inspector Mason to bring some pressure to bear on the buyer's London lawyers. They will likely know more than they'd be prepared to disclose to me. Unless they themselves are criminals, I suspect INTERPOL pressure could encourage them to divulge what they know, including in particular who they have been dealing with.'

'I like it, Tom. I'll ask Inspector Mason to consider speaking with you before he puts pressure on the London lawyer.'

'Thanks, Jason. I suggest we stick together and run the next phase of things from the business meeting room in the hotel on level 1. I've taken the liberty of booking it for the day.'

Willow called the waiter over and ordered each of them another barista coffee, without even asking. 'I was going to suggest exactly that. No sense in taking unnecessary risks by heading anywhere today. I'll contact Oliver Planksmith to bring him up to speed, and see if he can spare an extra body to help out. I'll also take up a secure position outside from which I can observe all entrances and exits to the hotel. I've charged our earpieces overnight and suggest we each wear them at all times, just in case.'

'Thanks, Willow.' Tom looked around from habit to make sure no one was within hearing range. 'I'll also need to contact my client to suggest they hold off signing the Terms Sheet until we nail down the legitimacy of the source of funds. That wasn't the original plan. I'll tell them we've come across a couple of irregularities that require further investigation, and that there is a need for some extra security. No sense in sharing all the details. Not at such a delicate stage in any event.'

The trio spent the remainder of the morning working through their respective allotted tasks, with varying levels of success.

Not unexpectedly, Tom found that Lorenzo Bassutri was away from the office for a few days. He thought it best to leave him to his own thoughts for now, and instead sent Lorenzo a brief email asking that he make contact when he felt up to it. The London lawyer was, however, particularly evasive, ignoring Jackson's calls and emails.

Jackson sent an email to his client asking them to hold off on signing the now finalised Terms Sheet until they were able to discuss the evolving situation.

Jones had more success with INTERPOL. He made contact with Inspector Wilfred Mason at UK INTERPOL, who was delighted to hear that Murray Jensen had been erased. Mason volunteered to bring Inspector Lachlan Darwin at Australian INTERPOL up to speed and to arrange a secure teleconference in the afternoon. In the meantime, he agreed to contact the buyer's London lawyer for information.

Willow had no trouble convincing her boss, Oliver Planksmith, to send another security operative to assist. He dispatched someone immediately and said they'd arrive early afternoon Italian time.

The three of them exchanged information over a light lunch, and readied themselves for the mid-afternoon secure teleconference with the inspectors from INTERPOL.

'I can't believe Murray Jensen is dead. You're absolutely certain, Jason?' Inspector Lachlan Darwin opened the conversation once the security and encryption protocols had been put in place. Jackson visualised the intent look on Darwin's face, his small brown eyes peering over the top of his spectacles perched on the end of his long, pointed nose.

'Absa-fucken-lutely.' Jones was smiling broadly. 'I'd recognise that nasty prick anywhere, even with an oddly crooked neck.'

'Then who killed him, assuming it wasn't the outcome of the hit and run accident as the Italian authorities are reporting it?' Inspector Mason queried.

Jackson imagined the portly London inspector rubbing the side of his very large nose, causing his thick grey moustache to twitch up and down.

'Very good question,' Jackson responded. 'We do have some theories, the strongest of which is that it is the re-emergence of the remnants of the Hong Kong-based syndicate. It might explain Murray Jensen's involvement and would certainly be consistent with the Chinese-accented woman seeking advance commercial information from our Italian lawyers. Did you have any luck convincing the London lawyer to cooperate?'

'As a matter of fact, I did. I have had previous dealings with the pompous little fellow, and it was almost as if he had been expecting my call. He had already received funds into the law firm's trust account in the amount of €200 million from two separate Swiss bank accounts. He mentioned that he had been unable to satisfy his own enquiries about the beneficial ownership and legitimacy of the money. I have formally frozen those funds, pending their likely confiscation under the anti-bribery and corruption laws. It didn't take much of a threat to his and his firm's professional standing to convince him to cooperate fully with us.' Jackson could hear that Inspector Mason was feeling pleased with himself.

'So was he able to provide you with details of his client?' Jackson was leaning forward in his seat, staring at the conference speaker in the centre of the table.

'He didn't have a choice really, although not before procuring the consent of the firm's managing partner. His client is Ping Xiaoyan, one of the two Hong Kong-based syndicate members who evaded capture last year.'

'Holy crap.' Jason Jones stood up and moved over to the window. 'It doesn't make any sense. If Jensen was working with Ping Xiaoyan, why kill him? Unless…'

'What, Jason?' Tom had witnessed Jason's analytical mind at work on many occasions, and was happy to let the process unfold.

'Well, either Jensen had gone rogue and was looking to exact some kind of unsanctioned revenge on us, or there is a third party or parties involved we have not yet identified, or a combination of both.'

'What makes you think he was in the process of taking revenge?' Darwin chimed in.

'Ah, good question, Lachlan,' Jones responded. 'I've thought a lot about what took place on the bridge yesterday. The only possible conclusion is that Murray Jensen had positioned himself and the operative I was following to abduct me again. He could've been planning to put some kind of pressure on you, Tom, in respect to the transaction in question, or simply to lure you to a location where he could deal with both of us at the same time. Perhaps in time, both. Given that we now believe the money from Switzerland is dirty money, my guess is that the abduction was initially to apply pressure to Tom. Who knows what he had in mind after that. It could be that the action was unsanctioned by a third party who has an interest in the funds that were being laundered, resulting in them reacting decisively and taking Jensen out.'

'Why is there necessarily a third party? Couldn't the funds belong to the syndicate?' Darwin again.

'You could be right,' Jones continued. '€200 million is a lot of mula, and six months is not much time for the syndicate to regroup and have access to that amount in Swiss bank accounts. Remember that on two previous occasions we know of, the syndicate's funds came from tax havens in the Caribbean Islands.

What tends to convince me that a third party is involved is the decisive manner in which Jensen was terminated. I can't see the syndicate getting rid of Jensen given their history, and particularly not while such large sums are in play. On the other hand, I can see a third party doing so if Jensen had, for example, ignored any warnings to put personal vendettas to one side for now.'

'How will we know for certain?' Tom lowered his voice.

'I can answer that one,' Inspector Mason piped up. 'Word about confiscation of the funds will quickly flush out the owner. If we are on the right track here, then more public displays of their displeasure, not unlike the ruthless manner in which they dealt with Jensen, are a distinct possibility. Tom, the threat to you, Jason and anyone else in your party is real. You might need to think about beefing up your security and relocating.'

'Inspector, it's Willow Douglas here. A second security operative from our team in London joined us not long ago and has taken over responsibility for external cover. That means we now have three professionals with Tom. I agree we need to relocate soon, and prior to formal confiscation of the funds if at all possible.'

Jackson spoke after a brief pause. 'Thanks all. We'll get back to you with a plan shortly. Any further comments at this time?' As there were none, he ended the call.

Chapter 22

Luna Smythe, Ping Xiaoyan and Yen Chow Yu had checked out of both their hotels and relocated to a two-bedroom apartment just beyond the southern outskirts of Rome. The apartment had in the past served as a safe house for Murray Jensen's operations in the region.

'I've just had a brief call with our London lawyer. Initially he refused to take my call. I had to threaten his personal assistant to get him to speak with me.' Xiao had been staring out the window, looking at the green rolling hills in the distance. She turned slowly. 'You're right, Luna. We are fucked. INTERPOL has frozen the Swiss funds that were already in the lawyer's trust account. Confiscation is the likely outcome. The lawyer told me that was the last time he would communicate with me. The mafia and the drug cartel will both be furious.'

'So where to from here?' Yu always liked to have next steps mapped out.

'I have access to Murray's private jet. I don't know exactly where it is, but I do know that it is somewhere in Europe, no more than one hour's flight away. I set up Murray's secure global communication network, and my administrative privileges give me access to all the key codes and commands.' Luna was twisting the dress ring on the index finger on her right hand.

'Let's not be too hasty.' Xiao had returned her gaze to the view outside. 'Fantastic that we have a convenient means of escape though. Luna, I suggest you alert the pilot to our immediate need and have him head our way for an extraction later today. You can sort out the logistics of where. In terms of when, let's make it not before eight p.m.'

'So what's our plan in the intervening period?' Yu was more than happy to defer to Xiao on all matters now that he was aware of her true lineage.

'I was thinking we might head over to Jackson's hotel and take out both him and Jones. Luna, we'll leave you here to finalise all arrangements for our departure this evening. Let me know if there are any issues.'

It was late afternoon when Xiao and Yu arrived at Jackson's hotel. It didn't take them long to spot Oliver Planksmith's second operative. He was well hidden to the casual observer, but his fatigue had made him a little lax in a professional sense. Yu seemed impressed that Xiao spotted him first. 'I'll deal with that one. You stay here.' Xiao was already on the move before the surprised Yu could say anything.

Yu watched as Xiao expertly snuck up on the Planksmith security operative. She produced a ceramic ice pick from her boot in a practised move and embedded it in the surprised operative's carotid artery. He collapsed in a heap in her arms, and she expertly lay him on his side, as if he were sleeping.

'I've seen that manoeuvre before,' Yu whispered to Xiao when she returned, clearly impressed.

'Let's just say Madeline, the one you know as the ghost, and I had the same teacher.'

*

'Our new colleague has missed his scheduled call.' Willow was shaking her head as she raised the alarm with Jackson and Jones.

They had been working through next steps themselves, and had resolved to head to London at the first available opportunity. The second buyer, their advisers and their financier were all located in London. Jackson knew that, while the terms were not as favourable as those in the now defunct Terms Sheet, it was already shaping up to be a deal with more normal parameters associated with it. Apart from anything else, the buyer was an entity listed on the London Stock Exchange.

'When did he last check in?' Jones was on his feet, automatically checking his weapon.

'Fifteen minutes ago from the north-eastern quadrant.' Willow was also checking her weapon as she moved towards the door. 'I'll head to the roof now to see if I can spot him.'

'Roger that. Tom and I will wait here until you advise. Comms are still active.'

'I'm on the roof, and I see my colleague. He's on his side, positioned as if he's sleeping. He's not. He's down. On my way back to you now.'

'Fuck! We're a little cornered here, with only one way in and one way out. Head to reception and we'll meet you there.' Jones had grabbed Tom's elbow and was leading him to the stairs.

Jackson had removed the Swiss army knife from his pocket and exposed the largest blade. 'You lead. I'm right behind you.'

Jackson and Jones emerged from the stairwell into reception at the same time as Xiao and Yu rushed through the entrance. They almost collided. Yu raised his silenced gun to fire at point blank range into Jackson's chest. Tom's instincts kicked in and he dodged to his left as the gun fired. At the same time as moving to the left he slashed down with his sharp blade, cutting deeply into the arm carrying the gun. Yu cried out in pain and immediately dropped the gun.

Yu's pained roar momentarily distracted Xiao, who was lunging at Jones with her ceramic ice pick. Tom had moved into Jason's line of fire. Instead of firing his gun, Jones launched a powerful kick at Xiao's outstretched hand, instantly snapping the ceramic ice pick in half. A split second later he delivered a second kick from his other leg to the same hand. It was met with a cracking sound signalling a broken bone in Xiao's hand. Xiao's involuntary grunt of pain confirmed this. A third kick from Jones to the side of Xiao's head dropped her to the floor like a sack of potatoes.

Jackson overpowered the wounded Yu and had him on the floor in a vicious headlock. He looked up to see Willow Douglas charge into reception from the stairwell. Her gun was drawn and she was expertly sweeping it from side to side, ready to fire.

'I wouldn't if I were you, signora.'

Those who were conscious swivelled their heads as one to the sound of the voice. Standing in the entrance to the reception area were two very large Italian men, their guns drawn and also sweeping from side to side, covering the scene before them.

'We have no quarrel with you, signora.' The smaller of the two men standing in the entrance spoke with a thick Italian accent. 'Our instructions are to acquire Signore Yu and Signora Xiao and deliver them to il grande capo, the big boss, for questioning. Disarm your captives and surrender them to us and we will leave. No harm will come to you.'

Tom, Jason and Willow exchanged glances, and nodded to each other. Willow maintained her vigilance, sweeping her gun expertly from one newcomer to the other, while Tom and Jason handed the restrained Xiao and Yu over to the Italians. Xiao had recovered remarkably quickly from the blow to her head. The man who spoke holstered his weapon and used cable ties to properly restrain their captives.

*

Xiao and Yu were forcefully directed towards a van waiting around the side of the hotel, away from the nearby permanent police presence. As they approached the empty van, Xiao dislocated her thumb on her injured right hand and slipped the cable ties off. Yu saw what was happening and struggled a little harder to create a distraction for Xiao. In one swift movement, Xiao forcefully dug the thumb of her uninjured left hand into the pressure point below her captor's ear, instantly rendering him unconscious. She repeated the process to the other unsuspecting captor as he spun to see what had happened to his colleague.

Xiao located a knife on one of the fallen men and freed Yu, who then collected the fallen men's guns. As he pointed a gun at one of the men, Xiao stopped him. 'We will leave them alive. It's one thing to deprive the mafia of their money, but another thing entirely to kill one of their numbers. They are all related in one way or another. Retribution for killing a family member is pursued relentlessly. We'll take their van to get out of here quickly, and ditch it on our way back to Luna. Who knows what tracking devices they may have on their vehicles. Once we patch ourselves up, we can disappear with Luna on the private jet.'

Chapter 23

'That was close!' Jackson was breathing heavily.

Willow had returned after having carefully followed the Italian pair and their captives outside. 'You won't believe what happened once they were outside.'

'Try me.' Jones was also breathing heavily, more from relief than exertion.

'The Chinese woman managed to free herself somehow, and within seconds had immobilised the two Italians. She touched each on the neck and they dropped to the ground as if overcome by some magic spell. She freed her colleague and they took off in a van that was parked around the corner.'

Hotel reception staff were emerging from the hiding spots they had flung themselves into when the melee began. 'Are you okay, signors and signora? I have summoned the nearby polizia to assist.' The hotel manager replaced the reception phone as he straightened his uniform.

'Grazie.' Jackson was again on alert. The last thing they needed was to be detained by authorities pending an investigation.

Jones moved over to Willow with his back to the hotel staff, and handed her his gun. 'Take this, Tom's knife and your gun and hide them in the meeting room. Then get back here pronto, so we can deal with the police enquiries together.'

'Mi scusi, excuse me. I need a quick toilet stop after that.' Willow left quietly via the stairs.

Willow returned just as two police officers arrived, accompanied by the now conscious Italian pair. To Tom's surprise, the police and the two men were chatting animatedly in a relaxed manner. It was almost as if they knew each other. It suddenly dawned on him that the Italian pair must be members of the mafia. What had they said? They were taking Ping Xiaoyan and her Chinese colleague to il grande capo, the big boss. Maybe the third party they had been talking about was the Italian mafia. He wondered if they were in cahoots with the police.

Jackson's thoughts were interrupted when the smaller of the two who had taken the Chinese pair spoke. 'Signors and signora, I have just been explaining to our friendly law enforcers that it has all been a huge misunderstanding.' He was glaring at the hotel staff, as if to warn them not to say otherwise. 'We had a disagreement with a man and a woman who have now left. No one has been injured and there is no harm done.'

The hotel manager had taken the hint. 'Si, it was all just a harmless scuffle with a bit of name calling. I apologise profusely for involving busy officers of the law.' The manager spoke in very clear English with his head bowed slightly.

The police officers nodded to each other and left without taking any details whatsoever of the dangerous events that had taken place only moments ago. Tom saw the smaller Italian man shake hands with the hotel manager and slip an envelope into his jacket pocket. Money for silence, and perhaps to repair the bullet hole in the wall, wherever it may be.

'We will go and see if we can relocate our friends,' the smaller man said as the pair smiled and turned to leave.

Tom, Jason and Willow regrouped in the meeting room.

'Okay, so the third party we have been theorising about does exist, and it's the Italian mafia.' Jones had slipped into one of the lounge chairs in the meeting room.

'My thoughts exactly.' Jackson had taken a nearby seat.

'We're not out of the woods yet.' Willow had remained standing. 'My immediate concern, however, is to check on my colleague outside. If I'm correct and he has been killed then we need to quietly repatriate his body home.'

'Spot on, Willow. You go and check, and I'll call Oliver now. I'm sure he will have someone local who can assist us with this.' Jones was already dialling Planksmith's number.

'Roger that.' Willow left and within moments had confirmed on comms that her colleague was deceased.

'Did you catch that, Jason?' Tom whispered to Jones, who was speaking with Oliver Planksmith. Jones nodded and kept talking to Planksmith.

'Willow, do you copy?' Jones had ended the call with Oliver.

'Copy.'

'I have spoken with Oliver, and he'll have someone to your location within thirty minutes to remove your fallen colleague's body. He's absolutely gutted by the loss, and will speak with next of kin. Once the body has been collected, we'll need to call Oliver again and give him a more fulsome update.'

'Roger that.'

Tom and Jason were still discussing the events of the morning when Willow returned. 'One thing I'll say about Oliver, he has amazing connections. My colleague's body has been collected and will be taken to a private morgue, before repatriation to London later today on a charter flight.'

They called Oliver Planksmith on the conference phone and spent the next forty-five minutes bringing him up to speed on recent events. Willow had not mentioned all the details in her chat with Oliver that morning.

'It looks like you have a tiger by the tail, again. Perhaps even the same tiger.' Oliver had been listening intently to the three of them and asking questions where he required clarification. 'I can't believe Murray Jensen is dead. I'm not unhappy about it, just a little surprised. I'm inclined to agree with your collective analysis that the remnants of the Hong Kong-based syndicate are in operation and again plying their money laundering trade. The Italian mafia are also likely involved. The fact that they had captured

Ping Xiaoyan and her Chinese colleague and were planning to take them to il grande capo for questioning tells me they have skin in the game. It's not really their style, however, to carry out a very public execution in central Rome. They're usually more subtle when it comes to killings on their home turf. That could mean that there is yet another unidentified party involved.'

'That's about where I got to, Oliver, except the bit about the extra party. I don't have your knowledge of the mafia's modus operandi when it comes to killings on home turf.' Jones was again pacing the room. 'Needless to say that anyone involved with the deal will be severely pissed off as soon as they learn that INTERPOL is planning to confiscate the €200 million. We could soon have the remnants of the Hong Kong-based syndicate, the Italian mafia and an unidentified but ruthless party hunting for us.'

'Holy fuck!' The realisation of the seriousness of the position they were in was making Tom's head spin. 'We need to leave, pronto.'

'Spot on,' Oliver jumped in. 'I suggest you hire a non-descript vehicle using one of Willow's fake IDs and head north. There are more than thirty smaller airports in Italy. I'll send a private jet to one of them and will call you with details when I've made the arrangements.'

The three of them packed, but did not formally check out of the hotel. They were paid up for another few days and wanted to have a head start on any bad guys who came back to the hotel looking for them. Tom and Jason managed to sneak their luggage past hotel reception staff while Willow hired a vehicle and met them outside.

It was well into the evening when Jackson and his colleagues boarded a private jet at a regional airport north of Rome, bound for London.

Little did they know that earlier in the evening, Ping Xiaoyan, Yen Chow Yu and Luna Smythe had boarded Murray Jensen's private jet at a regional airport south of Rome.

Chapter 24

DAY 9 (Tuesday)

Matteo Ricci sat upright in one of the four chairs in his small office in Via Cassia in central Rome. As head of operations for the Sicilian mafia in Rome, he was not accustomed to being disciplined or threatened in any way. He had an uneasy feeling as he faced his immediate superior, Alfonso Rossa, and the head of security for the Colombian drug cartel, Pablo Barato. A man of imposing bulk himself, it was rare for Ricci to feel intimidated. And yet his instinct was to cower before the two men opposite. He knew the reputation of both, and could only hope that he did not betray his true internal feelings.

Pablo Barato addressed both Ricci and Rossa in a deep, controlled voice, and in perfect English. 'So then, as I understand it, you not only unwisely gave in to the demands of the Chinese woman, Ping Xiaoyan, to surveil the lawyer, Tom Jackson, you sent a pair of imbeciles to do so.' He held up his oversized calloused hand to signal that he did not wish either of his listeners to interrupt. 'Your people were discovered on two occasions and on the third, they killed a young innocent lawyer as she came out of the toilet in a very public place. Sending both to their maker does absolutely nothing to undo the damage they had already done. The next cock-up was that neither of us was able to persuade the reactive and irrational Murray Jensen to defer seeking satisfaction

116

for his personal vendetta against Tom Jackson and Jason Jones. In dealing with Jensen, we lost one of our best resources, but it had to be done.'

Matteo Ricci felt a chill run through him as he observed the look in Barato's cold dark eyes when he spoke about the brutal execution of Murray Jensen in broad daylight in central Rome.

'To top it off, you then sent two of your so-called best field operatives to apprehend the Chinese pair, Ping Xiaoyan and Yen Chow Yu, and they failed miserably.' Barato stood and kicked his chair back, knocking it heavily into the wall. He was six foot six, and towered over the two mafia representatives who had remained seated. 'The authorities in London have frozen our €200 million, and it is likely that it will be confiscated. We lose all of our money and you get nothing. Is that a good fucking summary of recent events?'

'I'm afraid it is.' Alfonso Rossa was glaring at Matteo Ricci. 'How can we make this right?'

'Exactly the right question.' Barato's breathing regularised and the visible tension in his shoulders dissipated as he resumed his seat. 'It's your mess, and you need to clean it up. You need to deal with Xiao and Yu, as you call them, as we have dealt with Murray Jensen.'

'They may have already left the country.' Ricci was squirming in his seat.

'Not my problem. Deal with it or we will. If we have to, we will not be interested in working with you on anything at all in the future. Oh, and one other thing. Tom Jackson and his colleagues are not to be harmed. If they are, it will cause the authorities to ramp up their enquiries into the origins of the confiscated funds. It's one thing to lose €200 million, which fucking hurts. It's another thing entirely to have our entire stash exposed. If we go down, so too will your Swiss-based operations. Do I make myself clear?'

'Crystal clear,' Rossa said calmly, and then through clenched teeth. 'Sort this shit out, Ricci, and don't fuck it up. You need to track down Xiao and Yu rapido, and eliminate them before they harm Jackson or anyone associated with him. I don't care about Jensen's missing tech analyst. She's harmless, although if she's now working with Xiao and Yu, take her out too.'

Pablo Barato stood and headed for the door. 'This meeting's over. I expect daily reports as a minimum, and more frequently as things ramp up.' He turned to glare at both of them. 'And don't make a permanent enemy of me.'

'We need to sort this out quickly, Matteo.' Alfonso Rosso spoke as soon as the door had closed. He and Matteo Ricci were second cousins and childhood friends. Matteo knew that Alfonso's aggression towards him in the meeting had been nothing more than a display for Barato.

'Agreed. I'll start with Xiao's hotel to see if they might know where they've gone, and then see if I can pick up the trail from where they abandoned the van they took from our colleagues.' Matteo had stood to eyeball his superior. They had grown up together and then risen through the ranks of the mafia at a similar pace through equally violent methods. It was only a small twist of fate that had resulted in Alfonso occupying the superior position. It hadn't altered their friendship, nor their unqualified support for each other.

'Let me know if you need any more resources.' They shook hands, and Alfonso left.

Ricci summoned his two henchmen who had been unsuccessful in their attempts to capture the Chinese pair. 'I've been told in no uncertain terms by our South American friends that Xiao and Yu must be tracked down and eliminated, and before they harm Jackson or any of his associates. If Jensen's tech expert Luna Smythe is working with Xiao and Yu, make her a pair of concrete shoes as well. Otherwise, leave her be.'

'Understood, boss,' the smaller of the pair responded squeezing his hands at his sides. 'I've been thinking about where they might have headed after they abandoned our van. They were definitely headed south. I'll lean on our contacts to see if the nearby traffic cameras can shed any light on their next mode of transport.'

'Okay. Keep me posted. I'll circulate photographs to our air-port-based contacts to see if anyone recognises them. Let's reconvene here later today to compare notes and work out next steps.' Matteo stood to signal that the meeting had ended, and his two henchmen sauntered out.

By later that day, Matteo Ricci had established that Jackson and his colleagues had flown out of an airport north of Rome in a private jet on Monday evening, destination London. He had tracked Xiao and Yu to an airport south of Rome and had confirmation they also flew out late Monday in a private jet. Frustratingly, no flight plan was recorded so he had no idea where they were headed. He reasoned that since Xiao and Yu had been interrupted in their attempts to kill Jackson and his colleagues in their hotel, they were more than likely also on their way to London to complete the task.

The mafia was well resourced and had its own fleet of private jets. Ricci tasked his two henchmen to head to London immediately and locate and protect Tom Jackson and Jason Jones. He was certain they would not have to wait long for the vindictive Chinese woman and her offsider to show up.

Chapter 25

Late on Monday, the jet carrying Xiao, Yu and Luna Smythe touched down at their hastily arranged destination near Nice in southern France. Xiao's instinct had been to head to London, as she was certain that's where Jackson and his colleagues would be heading. Smythe had insisted that she had no intention of returning to the United Kingdom. She had escaped from low-security custody six months ago and subsequently aided Murry Jensen in his escape while in transit to a maximum-security facility. Xiao was inclined to agree that there would be no low-security custody for Luna if she was captured again in that country.

As a compromise, Luna had agreed to authorise the pilot to travel to Nice for an overnight stopover. The jet would then be made available to Xiao and Yu for a flight to London.

They had checked into the Raddison Blu Hotel on Promenade des Anglais in Nice late in the evening. The hotel was at near capacity, so there were only two rooms available. A single and a twin. Yu took the single and Xiao and Luna agreed to share the twin room.

'I hope you don't mind sharing a room.' Xiao flung herself onto the larger of the two beds in the room.

'Not at all. It's only for one night.' Luna looked exhausted.

'I'll shower first.' Xiao was on her feet removing her clothes. She wriggled out of her loosely fitting long white linen shirt and peeled off the skin-tight full black body stocking she had been wearing underneath. Xiao never wore underwear. She observed herself in the full-length mirror on the front of the wardrobe, checking for bruising from their encounter earlier in the day. The tight strapping on her right hand secured her thumb, which had been broken by the kick from Jones. She stretched and clenched her fingers, satisfying herself that the broken thumb would not limit the range of movement to any great extent.

Out of the corner of her eye she could see that Luna was watching her, and was surprised to see her appreciative look. Thinking that she may have underestimated Luna's versatility, Xiao turned to face her. Luna maintained eye contact for a prolonged period before allowing her own eyes to wander over Xiao's nakedness. Xiao knew that she had an appealing physique, honed by her many hours of workouts and training over the years. Her small pointed breasts had been described by past lovers as exquisite. When Luna's eyes again met hers, Xiao couldn't help noticing her suggestive look. Luna's legs opened slightly as she lay on her bed.

As Xiao moved towards her, Luna sat up and began removing her blouse. Xiao helped Luna stand, before kissing her hungrily on the mouth. Their tongues explored each other's. While kissing, Xiao reached around behind Luna and unfastened her bra, exposing her full breasts. They were the colour of fresh snow, untouched by sun. As Xiao cupped her hand over one of Luna's breasts, she let out a low moan. Xiao lowered her head and teasingly kissed the nipples of both breasts, before removing Luna's long pants and brief underwear.

They stood naked together, caressing and kissing each other, before Xiao pushed Luna onto the bed. Xiao was well aware that she knew exactly how to pleasure another woman. She'd had plenty of experience doing so. Over the course of the next hour, Xiao applied all her skills, extracting moans and giggles from Luna on an almost continuous basis. She also patiently showed Luna how to reciprocate.

Afterwards they lay on the bed together, breathing heavily and covered in perspiration. 'How about that shower now?' Xiao asked.

'Together?' Luna responded with a wicked look in her eyes, licking her lips in an exaggerated manner.

Now morning, Xiao and Luna had met up with Yu in the hotel's breakfast area. Yu had arrived first and had selected a table as far away as possible from other guests.

'I've been in touch with our European connections overnight,' Yu began eagerly. Xiao nodded for him to continue, certain in her own mind that she had experienced a far more enjoyable evening than Yu. 'You were absolutely correct on where you thought Jackson and his group might head. They touched down at London Stansted Airport late yesterday.'

'Well done. Any idea where they went from there?' Xiao was looking over the lip of her cup while she sipped her green tea.

'Not yet. I'm working on it.' Yu seemed pleased to receive praise from Xiao.

'I might be able to help with that.' Luna did not look up from the cooked breakfast she was devouring. 'I'll contact Murray's third-party connections in London to see if they can establish Jackson's whereabouts from CCTV camera networks.'

Xiao could see that Luna was as hungry as she was after their nocturnal activities. 'That would be helpful. While you are doing that, can you direct your pilot to take us to a smaller airfield in the UK, so that we can arrive as undetected as possible?'

'No problem. Give me an hour or so after breakfast to arrange the flight. It might take me a little longer to trace the whereabouts of Jackson.'

'Okay. The sooner the better. You can communicate with us about Jackson's location while we are enroute.' Xiao intentionally maintained her authoritative voice. It was time to focus on the tasks ahead. Not just the elimination of Tom Jackson and Jason Jones, but on what came after that.

*

At around the same time, Tom Jackson, Jason Jones and Willow Douglas were enjoying a chef-made breakfast at one of Oliver Planksmith's safe houses in London. Planksmith had sent a car to meet the plane when it landed at Stansted. All had agreed that it would be safer to avoid any kind of public transport and to stay away from regular hotels.

The driver of the car was none other than Russell, the over-sized man of African descent who had provided assistance and protection to Tom on two prior visits to London. His beaming smile when he saw the trio, coupled with the knowledge that he was a Taekwondo Master, provided a measure of reassurance to each of them. Oliver had tasked Russell with being on standby no more than a two-minute drive away from wherever they might be. Tom knew Russell didn't need much sleep while on an operation.

'Here we go again,' Jackson said, sipping his mandatory cappuccino. 'I'll get in touch with Lorenzo Bassutri in Rome. He sent me an email late yesterday letting me know that he would be back in the office today. My client is also now aware that the first deal is a no go, and has authorised me to progress the back-up deal, with haste of course. Once they get their teeth into something, they don't give up until a resolution in their favour is reached.' Tom reflected for a moment that almost all of his clients shared this trait. Perhaps his professional attitude of getting everything done as quickly as possible, on time and on budget, attracted clients with similar attributes. Tom wouldn't have it any other way. What he could do without, however, was the constant threat of execution by seasoned criminals.

'While I progress this deal, I think we need to go on the front foot and address the threats we face head on.' Tom was rubbing his temples in thought.

'I hear you, and have been thinking the same thing,' Jones said, with a mouthful of eggs and toast. He stopped talking and swallowed his mouthful before continuing. 'As I said yesterday, once it becomes obvious that the first deal is not proceeding, and funds are confiscated, we will have a lot of unhappy people looking to exact revenge. I'll work with Oliver and Willow to establish a protective shield around us here, and also to issue alerts to be on the lookout for Ping Xiaoyan and her Chinese colleague, or Xiao and Yu as the mafia 'gentlemen' called them. We should be able to get INTERPOL to prevail on the Colonna Palace Hotel to share their security footage with us, and we can feed the details into the facial recognition capability associated with the extensive London CCTV network. I'm sure our mates at INTERPOL will be more than happy to assist. The prospect of snaring any remaining members of the syndicate will be irresistible. Dealing with the Italian mafia and whoever they may be working with is another matter altogether. One step at a time. Do you have what you need to work from here for now, Tom?'

'I do. The place is extremely well equipped with high tech office-related equipment. There's enough space for all of us in the large room set up as an office. If you'll excuse me, I'll get on with it.'

Chapter 26

Jones and Willow were quick to establish security protocols for their safe house location. Oliver Planksmith was happy to provide whatever resources they thought they might need. The safe house was located in a leafy part of the outskirts of southern London in Sundridge, just outside the M25 motorway. It was farther outside central London than most of Planksmith's other safe houses. Oliver had selected the location in the expectation that Tom Jackson would not need to attend many face-to-face meetings in central London. Tom had agreed that he should be able to achieve his ends through email communication and video conferencing when required. The lower density of population in the surrounding area would also make it easier to secure. Unwelcome visitors could be spotted before they were able to get too close to the house.

After a brief early morning call from Jones, Inspector Wilfred Mason from UK INTERPOL was able to open a channel of communication with his Italian counterparts. Management at the Colonna Palace Hotel had promptly made available their security footage of the parties involved in the violent scuffles in the reception area the day before. Mason had persuaded Italian INTERPOL to defer any formal investigations into the event, for now.

'Tom, I have Inspector Mason on the phone. Do you have time for a brief chat.'

'Of course, Jason.' Jackson stood up from his desk, happy to have an opportunity to stretch his legs. 'Good morning, Inspector.'

'Top of the morning to you, Tom.' Jackson thought Mason sounded uncharacteristically jovial, and so was expecting good news.

'Good news, I think,' the inspector began. Jackson winced a little at the words 'I think', but remained silent. 'With the assistance of our Italian colleagues we have managed to identify all four assailants involved in the incident in the hotel reception yesterday. The Chinese pair are Ping Xiaoyan and Yen Chow Yu, the two Hong Kong-based syndicate members who escaped our sweeping raids last year. The two large Italian men are both known enforcers for the Rome chapter of the Sicilian mafia. Italian INTERPOL impressed upon me how important it was to avoid any injury to the Italian gentlemen unless absolutely necessary. I was a bit surprised at their insistence on this and was unable to ascertain exactly why. All I can surmise is that there is a level of, shall we say, cooperation that exists between the Italian INTERPOL and the Sicilian mafia. It's not for us to query this, and we should endeavour to respect their wishes on this if we want to continue to work cooperatively with them.'

'If the Italians pose a threat to any of us, we won't hesitate to take the fuckers out.' Jones was glaring at the speaker phone in the centre of the table, his hands on his hips.

'Understood, of course, Jason,' Mason responded quickly. Tom visualised the inspector wrinkling his large nose in distaste at Jason's profanity. 'I'm completely with you on this. We will never understand how some of our foreign counterparts operate, althhough we must respect their stated wishes wherever possible.'

'Jason, Willow, please make sure that any unwelcome visitors are treated appropriately.' Jackson winked at Willow.

'I get it. We'll shoot the Chinese pair on sight, and ask nicely what the Italians are doing, and shoot them straight away if we're not happy with their answer.' Jason had folded his arms and was looking between Tom and Willow.

'Inspector, Willow Douglas here. I'll make sure my colleagues get the message. There's often only a split second to decide whether to pull the trigger or not. We'll do our best.'

'Thank you all. Now that you are secure in a safe house, we have decided to take the final step and formally confiscate the €200 million. That will no doubt poke the bears. Unless there is anything further, I'll sign off and get on with tracking down the whereabouts of at least the Chinese pair.'

Jackson and his colleagues said they had nothing further for the inspector and the call was ended.

'How the hell are we supposed to do that? Interview the Italian mafia enforcers before we engage? Risky as.' Tom could see that Jason was angry.

'As I said to the inspector, Jason, we'll do our best. We need to remember how things played out in the hotel reception in Rome. The Italians said they were only there to capture Xiao and Yu, and not to harm us.' Willow's smile wavered a little as she gently shook her head.

'Circumstances and instructions to enforcers can change.' Jason's arms remained folded.

'I hear you, Jason. You can accompany me to pass on appropriate directions to my three recently arrived colleagues outside.'

'Roger that.' Jones had unfolded his arms and headed to the door with Willow.

'I'll leave the two of you to sort all that out,' Jackson called after them, smiling at Jason's rigidity, and once again taking comfort from his presence. 'I have a call shortly with Lorenzo Bassutri.'

Jackson returned to his desk and dialled Bassutri's number in Rome

'Ciao, Signor Tom. I have been expecting your call. Apologies I was not in the office yesterday.' Lorenzo sounded tormented.

'I completely understand, Lorenzo. I am so very sorry for what happened to Francesca on Saturday.' Jackson chose his words with care, waiting until Lorenzo was ready to speak.

'Grazie, Tom. I confess I am still having difficulty processing what happened. What I saw.' Lorenzo was silent again for a moment. 'I thought it best to return to work and immerse myself in our deal. I see that the backup deal is now proceeding at pace. I assume the first one has come to an abrupt halt?'

'It has. I will let you have more detail when I'm able to. In the meantime, we need to crack on with the replacement deal.' Jackson was careful not to disclose too much information to anyone, although he had no particular reason to mistrust Lorenzo.

'Ah, si. I like this term "crack on".' Tom could hear that Lorenzo's mood had lightened a little.

The lawyers spoke for some time about the progress of the backup deal, and next steps. Once their respective tasks had been allocated, they agreed to end the call, and crack on.

*

Jason and Willow exited the safe house and spoke to each of the three concealed Planksmith operatives, careful to ensure that they did not attract any unwarranted attention while doing so. They distributed photographs of Xiao, Yu and the two Italian enforcers.

Jones found it difficult to pass on Inspector Mason's request to avoid harming the Italians if at all possible, and deferred to Willow on this. He reminded each operative that their safety, together with that of their colleagues and everyone in the safe house was paramount.

'If you see anything suspicious at all, call it in. If that suspicion turns into a real threat, do what you do best, whoever it is on the other end of your gun-sights.' Jones did not want there to be any confusion about what the priority was. Willow had said her piece, and he made sure to finish off each briefing. All three of the external security operatives had signalled their understanding with the mandatory 'Roger that'.

Jones and Willow returned inside to report to Tom that those outside had now been briefed. Willow left to separately report the current directives to Oliver Planksmith.

The remainder of the day was spent without incident, at least insofar as Jackson and his party were aware.

Chapter 27

DAY 10 (Wednesday)

Luna Smythe had successfully arranged for the private jet to take Ping Xiaoyan and Yen Chow Yu to a small airport north of London on Tuesday afternoon. While en-route, Luna had made contact with Xiao.

'We were able to track Jackson and his party leaving Stansted Airport on Monday evening. We tracked the car south on the M25 Motorway and lost it in the Dartford West Tunnel where it crosses under the Thames,' Luna began her report.

'Lost it. How so?' Xiao was focused and knew her voice would sound unfriendly.

'Not sure yet. It looks like there's a couple of cameras temporarily out of action on the M25 around that location. I have resources trying to pick up the trail.'

Xiao and Yu had stayed overnight in a boarding house in Bexleyheath, not far from Dartford, with the intention of resuming their hunt for Jackson and Jones once Luna had traced their next moves.

What they were unaware of was that Jackson's driver, Russell, had taken a deliberately circuitous route to the safe house in Sundridge. After leaving the Dartford West Tunnel, Russell had headed west, away from their final destination. He had driven to Lambeth, just south of central London, and parked in an underground garage to confuse any attempts to follow them. They had exchanged vehicles and departed thirty minutes later. Two other vehicles had exited the garage before them.

'Good morning, Xiao.' Luna had sounded happy when she picked up the phone the following morning. Xiao was hoping for better news. The longer they stayed in London, the riskier it became. She wanted to get rid of Jackson and Jones once and for all and return to Portugal to resume their global operations.

'What news?' Xiao was not in the mood to exchange pleasantries.

'We have managed to track Jackson's vehicle to an underground garage in a block of apartments in Lambeth. There is no record of the vehicle having departed, so they must be on site. Sending you the location and car details now.'

'Well done! We'll head there now. Have your pilot on standby at the same airport. If all goes according to plan, we'll collect you in Nice on our way to Portugal.' Xiao had a small evil grin as she ended the call. She turned to look at Yu, taking delight in the knowledge that her cobra-like stare would strike fear into the hearts of most. Yu did not disappoint, looking down almost immediately.

'Can you function with the injury to your arm?' she asked Yu, forcing him to resume eye contact.

'Absolutely. Luna located a first-aid kit in the hotel in Nice and helped me stitch and bandage the wound shortly after breakfast yesterday. I always have pain killers with me, and I've taken just enough to minimise pain without dulling my senses.'

'Good. Let's go and get our revenge.'

It didn't take them long to arrive at the location provided by Luna. They broke into the downstairs garage and located the vehicle in question. It was completely empty. A resident was heading to her car, and looked surprised to see the Chinese pair peering in the windows of the unfamiliar vehicle.

'Good morning. Is that your car?' she queried pleasantly.

'No. Do you know where the occupants might be?' Xiao was doing her best to control her anger.

'I've lived here for six months now and I've never seen that car before, sorry. It's a bit weird really.'

'Weird. How so?' Xiao was starting to lose her patience.

'Well, there was another unfamiliar car in the same car park yesterday, and now it's gone.' The resident continued to her vehicle, calling over her shoulder. 'Late for work. Sorry I couldn't assist.'

'Fuck. Car switch. Now we have no idea where they are.' Xiao dialled Luna Smythe's number as she and Yu left the carpark.

'Luna. They switched cars in the basement carpark. Can you track any vehicles leaving the basement after they arrived.' Xiao was shaking her head in frustration.

'On it.' Luna replied. 'I'll get back to you stat.'

Luna was back in contact fifteen minutes later. 'Update.' Xiao's one word reply was intended to convey her anger and frustration.

'Three cars left the underground garage within an hour of the arrival of Jackson's vehicle. Then nothing for another three hours.' Xiao could hear the dread in Luna's voice, although it was not her fault.

'Can you initiate a trace on all three.'

'Already underway. I have managed to rule out one, which returned later in the evening after a trip to a local restaurant. Still working on the other two.'

'Change of tack. While we wait on the results of those enquiries, can you see if you can identify either of those two Italian mobsters who captured us briefly in the hotel in Rome on Monday. It occurs to me that they might still be after us and may themselves have headed to London for that purpose. They might lead us to Jackson in their search for us.' Xiao was angry with herself not to have thought of that before.

'Will do. I'll also see if I can track any of Oliver Planksmith's operatives who have been on the move recently. It's highly likely Jackson will again enlist Oliver's assistance with security.'

'Good plan. Talk soon.' Xiao ended the call.

*

The two mafia enforcers had also arrived in London the day before. Their connections had been able to ascertain that Xiao and Yu's jet had travelled from Rome to Nice on Monday evening. They were aware that the jet had left Nice on Tuesday, although had not yet been able to trace the flight path.

The enforcers had spent the night in a hotel not far from Stansted Airport, their port of arrival. The smaller of the enforcers, Alfredo, was the more senior of the two, and had been waiting stoically for more information. Alfredo was in his mid-thirties, heavy set and wore his long hair in a pony tail. His offsider, Luigi, was a similar age and size. His bald head betrayed the fact that he was four inches taller than Alfredo. The pair presented as a formidable presence, and were often sent on missions together.

'Alfredo, Matteo here.'

'Yes, boss.'

'We have located Tom Jackson and his party. We have a contact in the Rome office of global law firm Andrich Wiley. He has been most helpful.'

Matteo Ricci provided his enforcers with the address of the safe house in Sundridge where Jackson and his colleagues were staying. Tom had unwittingly disclosed their whereabouts to Lorenzo Bassutri in their conversation the day before. Bassutri was related to senior figures in the Sicilian mafia, and had been persuaded that it was in Jackson's best interests if the mafia enforcers arrived before the vindictive Chinese pair. He was told that the enforcers were sent to protect Tom and his colleagues, and to eliminate the Chinese pair.

'We'll head there pronto, boss, and report.' The call ended, and Alfredo and his colleague made ready to leave, checking their inventory of weapons.

Chapter 28

The mafia enforcers parked their car several blocks away from the Sundridge safe house.

'Carry only concealed weapons for now, Luigi,' Alfredo directed his colleague. 'Let's scope the place to check on their security arrangements. From our drive by, it looks as if the safe house is well chosen, with plenty of clear space surrounding it, and nearby bushes and trees to conceal overwatch security.'

'Got it.' Luigi was concealing a hand gun in the belt at the small of his back, and another snub-nosed revolver in a holster at his ankle under his loose-fitting long trousers. A switchblade in his jacket pocket completed his arsenal.

Alfredo carried similar weaponry. They had decided to leave the sawed-off shotguns and Uzi sub-machine guns in the boot of their London-based chapter's SUV.

The Italian enforcers spotted two of the three Planksmith operatives who had taken up external watch over the safe house. The third was well concealed, high in the branches of an English oak, above thick surrounding bushes.

*

'This is three, I have eyes on two possible hostiles, approaching from the south.' External operatives one and two shifted their gaze in a southerly direction, and each tapped their earpiece once to confirm the sighting.

'Jones here. Have they spotted any of you?' Jason was quick to respond, holding up his hand for silence in their work room.

'The way they are moving it looks like one and two have been spotted. I'm in the clear. Instructions?'

'Chinese or Italian enforcers?' Jones did not wish to waste words during a live threat.

'Unmistakeably Italian enforcers,' Three responded.

'Hold fire until any threat becomes apparent. Three, any chance you can circle behind the pair to apprehend?'

'On it.' Three's comms went silent.

'Welcome to London, gentlemen.' The Italian pair spun in the direction of three's voice. 'Weapons down.'

'There's two of us and only one of you. Besides, we're not here to harm you, only others who might wish to harm you and those you protect.' Alfredo and his colleague stood their ground.

'Make that three of us, and only two of you.' Operatives one and two were quickly on the scene.

'I'll say it again. Weapons down.'

Alfredo nodded to his colleague and they both placed their guns on the ground.

'One, check for other weapons.' As first on the scene, three had taken charge.

'I can help you with that.' Alfredo unholstered his snub-nose and placed that on the ground, along with his switchblade. Luigi did the same.

'Step back two paces, and hands behind your heads.' Three was signalling to his colleague to check for other concealed weapons.

'Clear.'

'Thank you, gentlemen. Now let's go and have a chat. One and two, return to your posts. I've got this.' Three continued speaking, 'Headed your way, control, with two disarmed Italian enforcers.'

'Already on my way to you to assist.' Jones had explained to all in the work room what was taking place outside.

Jason and Willow took charge of the captured enforcers, with Jones directing the Planksmith operative to rejoin his colleagues on overwatch.

'This way, signors.' Jones directed the Italians into a front room in the house. Willow stood guard at the door, her specialist capabilities plain to see. Jones continued as soon as his captives were seated. He had remained standing, his gun trained on both. 'Why is it that you're here, and how were you able to locate us?'

'Ah, Signor Jones. Good to see you also.' Alfredo smiled as he clasped his hands behind his head. 'As I mentioned to you, Signor Jackson and your tall, pretty colleague in Rome on Monday, it is not our intention to harm you.'

'Then what's your business, and how did you find us?' Jones squared up his shoulders and widened his stance.

Alfredo held up both hands in mock surrender. 'I'll explain. Hear me out.' Jones nodded for him to continue. 'We are here to deal with the Chinese syndicate members, Ping Xiaoyan and Yen Chow Yu. Our instructions are to eliminate them before they cause any harm to you or any of your colleagues.'

Jones stole a quick glace in Willow's direction. She shrugged her shoulders in response, and maintained her vigilance.

'That didn't work out too well for you in Rome, did it?' Jason sneered at his captives.

'Unfortunate outcome, I agree. We will not underestimate the witch the next time we meet. That was different, however. Our directions then were to capture the Chinese pair, and take them to il grande capo for questioning. We have different directions now from our business partners to eliminate Xiao and Yu.'

'Wait. What? Who are your business partners?' Jones was not surprised to be hearing of yet another party in the mix, particularly not after Oliver Planksmith's assessment of the very brutal and very public execution of Murray Jensen in central Rome.

'All I am at liberty to disclose is that our business partners are a powerful organisation based in South America. Let's just say they are very persuasive in their methods.' Alfredo was involuntarily wringing his hands.

'The Italian mafia is in business with a South American drug cartel? Unbelievable.' Jones scratched his jaw as he shook his head.

'I have told you all I am able to on that front. Let's just say our lives depend on carrying out our directions pronto.'

*

Tom Jackson had joined the group, standing outside the door behind Willow, and had heard most of the exchange. 'So who told you we were here?'

'Ah, Signor Jackson. A good question. The information came from someone in the law firm you are dealing with. Someone who has your best interests at heart.'

'Shit, our position here is compromised.' Tom was looking past Willow to gauge Jason's reaction to the new information.

'I think not,' Alfredo continued. 'If you have any information on the whereabouts of Xiao and Yu, share it with us and we will locate them and complete our mission.'

'Jason, a word please. Willow, cover these two as if they were here to kill us, which they may be.'

Jones left the room and joined Tom in the work room located at the rear of the safe house.

'What do you think, Jason?'

'I'm not sure if I should believe them, but I do. It does make some sense. The original deal has been exposed and funds confiscated. Probably the last thing the bad guys want is to attract more attention from the authorities as a consequence of the killing of any of us, and in particular you. On the other hand, the Chinese criminals probably have nothing further to lose.'

'So we should just let them go?' Tom raised his eyebrows.

'Why not? We have a fresh location on Xiao and Yu, courtesy of Inspector Mason. If we share that with these two thugs, they can do their thing and rid the world of the remaining two known members of the Hong Kong-based criminal syndicate.'

'Mason will not be happy.' Tom wasn't sure that what Jason was proposing was the right thing to do. The suggestion was not without merit.

'Then let's not tell him.' Jones grinned.

In the absence of a response from Tom, Jones turned and headed back to the room, speaking into his comms as he did so. 'We are going to release our Italian friends, reunite them with their weapons, and share the recent knowledge we have on the whereabouts of the Chinese pair.'

Chapter 29

Ping Xiaoyan and Yen Chow Yu had waited outside the apartment building in Lambeth, pending a further update from Luna Smythe.

'What's taking her so long?' Xiao was almost frothing at the mouth in an uncharacteristic display of her mounting frustration. The muscles in her neck were taught with tension.

Xiao could have no idea that she would not be receiving any more information from Luna. The mafia had caught up with Luna Smythe in Nice, having traced Murray Jensen's jet to that location. The Colombian drug cartel had shared details of the plane. It had been an easy task to lean on local contacts to ascertain the hotel she was staying in. Once they discovered Smythe was actively working with the Chinese, the instructions from Rome had been clear. The hotel staff would locate Luna's body at some stage, and medical examinations would conclude that she had died of a sudden heart attack. It would be unlikely if anyone thought to order an autopsy, and even if they did, it was highly improbable that the injection point between her toes would be discovered.

'Heads up. We have company.' Yu was on the move, followed by Xiao.

Both experienced assassins, they had not been waiting out in the open. Each had instinctively settled on the same location, which provided both quick access to cover and multiple escape routes. In seconds they were concealed from the approaching vehicle.

'It looks like those two mafia goons we tussled with in Rome.' Xiao was checking the magazine in her gun. She also reflexively checked the position of the replacement ceramic icepick in her boot.

'Agreed. I'll circle around behind them, and we can trap them in the crossfire.' Yu was about to leave when Xiao stopped him.

'Keep the small one alive for questioning. We don't need the bald one.'

The Italians had parked at a strategic distance from the Chinese pair's vehicle. They carefully exited, one armed with a sawed-off shotgun and the other with an Uzi sub-machine gun, and took cover behind opened car doors.

While the Italian enforcers were surveying the scene and planning their next move, Yu had already taken up a position behind them. He soundlessly approached the enforcers and shot the bald one in the head with his silenced pistol. As Alfredo turned to face the unexpected threat, Yu shot him in the wrist. Alfredo dropped his gun as he cried out in pain.

Xiao was on the scene in an instant, looking around to make certain there were no witnesses. 'Put the dead one in the boot of their car, and take the other one over there for questioning. If he makes a noise, see that he shares the same fate as his colleague.'

Alfredo's eyes widened, and his contorted expression showed the level of pain he was experiencing.

Xiao knew that she had limited time within which to extract the information she required before the Italian passed out from pain or blood loss, or both. Xiao and Yu were both proficient in the art of torture, and it took them no time to force the smaller Italian to tell them what he knew.

'Kill him and squeeze him into the boot with his colleague. We can move the car into the basement carpark of the apartment block. From what that resident told us, no one will look too closely into it until the decomposition of our former Italian friends

140

gives them away. We'll be long gone before then.' Xiao was feeling buoyed with the knowledge of the whereabouts of Tom
Jackson and Jason Jones. She did wonder briefly whether the Italians were there to kill or capture them but told herself that was
irrelevant. They had likely burnt their bridges with the mafia and
would have to find another way forward with their business endeavours. She knew that Luna would be invaluable in that
process.

'Let's get on with this. It shouldn't take us long to get to Jackson's safe house in Sundridge. They won't be expecting us, and
the Italian was kind enough to describe the extent and location of
external overwatch security as well as the internal layout of the
house.' Xiao directed Yu to drive while she formulated a plan of
attack in her mind.

Ten minutes out from arrival at the safe house, Xiao explained
her detailed plans to Yu. He remained silent and nodded slowly,
clearly impressed, as he kept his attention on the road.

Their planning was for nothing. Xiao could see as soon as they
drove past the house that it was empty. Jackson and co must have
decamped for another location shortly after sending the Italians in
their direction. They parked around the corner, intending to return to the house and see if they had unintentionally left any clues
behind as to their next location. Xiao made a mental note to contact Luna Smythe to see if she could get them a list of Oliver
Planksmith's safe houses.

'Be on the alert for any remaining security operatives. Highly
unlikely they would have left anyone behind, but let's for now assume they have.'

*

They had.

Jones had not heard from the Italian enforcers by the time they
had hastily packed and were ready to relocate to another safe
house. As a precaution, he had asked security operative three to

remain on site, but in a different location. Jones was always hoping for the best and planning for the worst.

'Control, this is three.'

'Copy three. Any action?' Jones was on full alert.

'Affirmative. Our Chinese targets have arrived and are in the process of a cautious reconnaissance of the area. Instructions?'

'Do you have line of sight?'

'Affirmative. I have the Chinese male in the crosshairs.'

'Take him out.' Jones wasted no time. These pair were dangerous.

'Confirm direct hit. Head shot. The female target moved like a leopard as soon as she heard me fire, almost as if she sensed what was about to happen before it did. She's gone to ground.'

'Watch that one. She's ruthless, and very skilled.' Jones was picturing the scene, and working out the best way to keep the security operative safe.

'Copy. I have the high ground in the fork of a large tree. She will know where I am, but without a sniper rifle will not be able to get close enough to present as a threat to me.'

'Update as appropriate.'

'Roger that.'

Jones turned to Tom and Willow, who had been watching him intently. 'Xiao and Yu are at the safe house we just vacated. Overwatch three has taken out Yu with a headshot. Xiao has gone to ground. I'll pass on updates as I get them.'

'Shit, that means our Italian friends are likely no longer alive.' It was all moving too quickly for Jackson.

'I need to bring Inspector Mason up to speed. I think I'll wait until I hear...' Jones stopped talking and held up his hand for silence. After a brief pause, he responded. 'Roger that. Don't come here. Head back to Oliver's base when safe to do so. She's a cunning bitch that one and might just lay in wait until you lead her to us. No sense in taking that risk.'

Jones turned to the others. 'That was three. He thinks Xiao assessed the situation and has hightailed it out of there. You heard me tell him not to come here, in case she is waiting patiently for him to lead her to us. I'll give Inspector Mason a call now. Apart from anything else, there's up to three bodies to be dealt with.'

*

Xiao had taken her time to assess the situation at the safe house in Sundridge. She concluded there was absolutely no way she could safely approach the security overwatch in the fork of the tree and take him out. He had chosen his perch well and had a three sixty-degree killing field. Deciding that it was safer for her to leave, she left her fallen colleague behind and did so.

Chapter 30

DAY 11 (Thursday)

Wednesday had been another huge day, and Jackson and his party had turned in early after ordering in. Tom had kept working on a laptop in his bedroom.

Oliver Planksmith had deployed a replacement team of three security operatives to the new safe house, once he'd received an update report from his returning team member. He had waited on site until Inspector Mason was able to send a clean-up crew to pick up Yu's body. Planksmith's driver, Russell, had given the INTERPOL crew directions and access codes to the basement of the apartment complex in Lambeth where residents had reported two unknown vehicles to the local police. The bodies of the two Italian enforcers were retrieved and the two unwelcome vehicles removed.

'Believe it or not, I have been able to make good progress on the key documentation for the deal to sell the Italian theme park.' Jackson was washing down his second croissant with an orange juice. He had already consumed his regular morning cappuccino.

Jason Jones and Willow Douglas each looked up and nodded, before returning their attention to the remainder of the cooked breakfast before them.

They had relocated to another Planksmith safe house on the same side of London. It was in central Bromley, not far from the

Bromley South overland rail station. While the area was more densely populated, the detached house occupied a defensible position on the corner of a busy intersection.

'Will you excuse me, please. I need to make a call to Lorenzo Bassutri.' Tom stood, leaving Jason and Willow at the table.

'No problems, Tom. Until we catch that woman, or hear of her demise, be on guard and stay away from exposed windows.' Jones pressed his lips together.

Jackson nodded and walked to a room in the rear of the house that had been set up as the primary work room.

'Ciao, Lorrenzo. Not too early I hope?'

'Buongiorno, Signor Tom. Not at all. We are making good progress, no?'

'We are, thank you. I need to discuss something of a highly sensitive nature with you.'

'It was me, Tom.'

'What do you mean?'

'I told the mafia your location south of London. I was told you were in danger, and that they were sending specially trained experts to protect you. Did they?'

'Not really.' Jackson thought it best to contain his anger, and wait for an explanation. He sat back in his chair with his lips pressed tightly together. He knew it was someone in Andrich Wiley who told the mafia of his whereabouts. He assumed that Lorenzo may have written the details in a file note that was discovered by someone else. His last thought was that Lorenzo himself had disclosed the information.

'My apologies, Tom. I thought I was doing the right thing by you. I am closely related to a senior figure in the Sicilian mafia. We share a family, not a lifestyle or business methodology. He insisted that it was a life-or-death matter, and forbade me from warning you. I hope you are safe.'

'I am. It's my fault for sharing our whereabouts. Let's just stick to legal issues relating to the sale transaction.' Tom did not wish to sour the relationship at this critical stage of the deal. He resolved to revisit the issue once everything had been finalised.

'Si, and again, I am truly sorry. I meant well.' Bassutri continued after a brief silence, 'Have you had a chance to look at the most recent draft of the primary documents, along with my comments and suggested amendments?'

'I have, Lorenzo. I spent some time on it late yesterday and emailed my client. They have responded overnight with clear instructions. We are getting close. I understand the Terms Sheet will be signed today, and we're aiming to finalise and sign primary documents next week sometime. If all goes according to plan, completion will take place late next week or early the week after, once all conditions to completion are met or waived. The buyer's financier is all over it, and says funds should be available in time.'

*

Ping Xiaoyan had spent the night in low-level accommodation on the outskirts of northern London. She had paid cash and provided personal details from one of her many false passports. Xiao had made contact with the pilot of Murray Jensen's jet and made arrangements to return to Nice at first light. Neither had yet heard of Luna Smythe's demise.

'Have you heard from Luna?' Xiao was not one for pleasantries, and certainly not so early in the morning.

'Nothing since Tuesday. You?' The concern registered on the pilot's face was no doubt a consequence of the recent loss of his primary benefactor, followed by the loss of contact with his replacement.

'Nothing since yesterday morning. Let's head back to Nice and locate her.'

The flight to Nice was a little over two hours, and they arrived mid-morning. Their taxi ride to the Raddison Blu Hotel on Promenade des Anglais in Nice was uneventful, until they rounded the final corner. An ambulance was on site, accompanied by a heavy presence of gendarmes, French paramilitary police officers.

'Stop here,' Xiao commanded the driver, who skidded to a halt at the nearest kerb.

'You go and find out what is going on. I will wait here.' Xiao almost pushed the pilot out the door.

The pilot was back in less than five minutes, his face ashen. 'She's dead. Heart attack, apparently. They didn't find her until this morning when they gained access for cleaning. I overheard the gendarmes expressing surprise at the sophistication of the hardware they found in the hotel room, and frustration at the level of encryption in place. A forensic team with tech experts is on the way.'

'Back to the airstrip. Now.'

The taxi pulled out from the kerb and executed a U-turn to head in the opposite direction.

Xiao was scrolling through her iPhone. They had only travelled a few blocks when she issued a new command to the driver. 'Change of plan. Circle back to the Aparthotel Adagio Nice in Promenade des Anglaise.' She held up her hand to prevent any protest from the pilot, who closed his eyes and slowly shook his head from side to side.

They exited the taxi and checked into the hotel, taking two rooms. Xiao directed the pilot into her room and closed the door. David was a small man of English descent. He had grown accustomed to the lavish lifestyle that had been afforded to him as the personal pilot for a powerful crime figure such as Murray Jensen. He was a little overweight and was sweating profusely. His prematurely thinning ginger hair was plastered to his head.

'Why are we here?' the pilot asked quietly.

'Don't worry, David. There is no risk to your personal safety. I need you to fly me to my next destination. I'm just not sure yet where that is.' Xiao had taken a seat in the lounge chair. She was trying without success to appear less intimidating. 'Sit down and let's talk.'

The pilot sat down on the edge of a dining chair at a two-seater breakfast table, his hands clasped tightly together between his knees.

'Do you speak French, David?'

'Yes, why?'

'I need you to go back to the hotel where they found Luna's body. Tell the gendarmes that you worked for Luna and that you're there to pick up her belongings, including her laptop.'

'Why would they listen to me, and what proof can I provide that I work for her?'

'No questions. This is what I need you to do. I will accompany you, and wait nearby. I will be watching. We leave now.' As Xiao stood, she allowed the pilot to see the hand gun protruding from the holster strapped to her inner thigh. He rubbed his sweaty palms down the side of his trousers as Xiao dug her strong fingers into his right shoulder, directing him towards the door.

Xiao and the pilot took less that ten minutes to walk the five hundred metres to Luna's hotel. Deep in thought, Xiao took in the beauty of her surroundings. The milky azure blue sea was always a special sight. She could never work out why people found it comfortable to hobble across the smooth irregularly shaped grey stones to a deck chair, and from there to the Mediterranean each time they wanted to immerse themselves in the buoyant salty water.

'You go in. I'll wait here, and no mistakes. If you encounter any resistance from the gendarmes, offer to come back at a later time to collect Luna's things. Keep them talking as long as you sensibly can, but make sure you are able to extricate yourself.'

Xiao waited until the pilot had reached the front of the hotel and begin conversing with the gendarmes. They were smiling at whatever it was that he had said by way of introduction. *Good.*

She crossed the busy road and made her way around to the back of the hotel. Her timing was perfect. One of the cleaners was exiting the rear door to take rubbish to a large skip bin. Xiao quickly immobilised her, dragging her back into the building and stealing her uniform, which she put on over the top of her clothes. After she hid the unconscious cleaner, she made her way quietly up the fire stairs to the room she had shared intimately with Luna two short days ago.

Xiao was relieved to see that the room itself was not guarded. The door was locked but it was no trouble for her to gain entry. With some relief she saw that Luna Smythe's body had been removed. She closed Luna's sophisticated laptop, gathered the three external hard drives and associated connected cables, and placed them in the shoulder bag Luna had used for that purpose. Xiao exited the room, descended the stairs and reclothed the still unconscious cleaner on ground level, leaving the building as quietly as she had arrived. As far as she could tell, she had not been observed by anyone. She had immobilised the cleaner from behind and had been careful to avoid exposure to any of the security cameras at the hotel.

Once Xiao was across the road, she caught the pilot's eye and signalled for him to join her. He bade his farewell to the gendarmes. As he approached her, she could see the surprised look on his face when he saw the laptop carry case over her shoulder. She gave him a rare smile as she patted the bag and turned to head back to their hotel.

Chapter 31

Jason Jones was on the phone to Inspector Mason from UK IN-TERPOL.

'We've heard from our Italian counterparts that Luna Smythe is deceased. She has been found in a hotel room in Nice.' Mason was puffing, as if he had been on a brisk walk. He hadn't. He was merely overweight and had stood from his desk chair to stretch his legs.

'When did this happen?' Jones was also on his feet, and beginning to pace across the work room. Tom and Willow had stopped what they were doing and directed their attention to their surprised colleague. Jones activated the speaker mode on his phone, and told Mason he was doing so.

'Smythe was found this morning. Preliminary indications are that she may have died up to twenty-four hours ago. The reason Italian INTERPOL is involved is because they were tracking a mafia enforcer who had travelled to Nice yesterday, and had alerted their French counterparts. The French are reasonably certain that Smythe died from natural causes, and had decided to mention the death to their colleagues as a courtesy.'

'So there's a possibility that the mafia has killed Murray Jensen's tech expert? That would certainly be consistent with what happened with the mafia enforcers here in London yesterday.' Jones told Mason he had shared the location of Xiao and Yu with the Italian enforcers. As Jackson predicted, the inspector was not happy. Jason knew that his reaction would have been very different if the enforcers had bested the Chinese pair. They hadn't.

'Quite likely, I'd say. I have strongly recommended an autopsy, although both the French and Italians are resisting, saying it will make things more complicated than they need to be.'

'Inspector, Jackson here. I'm inclined to agree with the French and Italians. Establishing Smythe's death as a murder will result in the need for an investigation. We know that Italian INTERPOL, and possibly also the French, have what appears to be a working relationship with the mafia. From our perspective, the mafia look to be consistently working in our best interests, against the Chinese pair. I would not like to interrupt that arrangement at such a critical time.'

'Very well then. There is some sense in what you say, although it does go a little against the grain. Perhaps we can revisit that at a later date.'

'Absolutely, Inspector,' Jones added quickly before he could change his mind.

'There has been no sign of Ping Xiaoyan. She has simply disappeared. I have facial recognition software scanning public transport and all major airports. We'll find her. She can't hide forever. I'll let you all get back to what you were doing. Just thought I'd bring you up to speed with the latest.'

'Roger that, Inspector.' Jones ended the call.

*

Xaio had set up Luna Smythe's laptop as soon as she returned with the pilot to her hotel. Xiao was brilliant with computers and it hadn't taken her long to unlock Luna's laptop. The intimate pillow talk the pair had shared had been very helpful. What was more difficult, however, was determining the codes required to access the secure global network that Smythe had set up for Murray Jensen.

'Maybe I can help with that.' The pilot had been sitting quietly in the corner, no doubt contemplating his fate. He spoke up when he heard Xiao express her frustration at not being able to determine the complex matrix of control codes.

'Do you have expertise in hacking into computer networks?' Xiao sneered at the pilot.

David continued, ignoring her jibe. 'No, but I spent some time on the plane with Luna and Murray, and I overheard them discussing the codes on numerous occasions.'

With the pilot's specific details, and Xiao's knowledge and understanding of computers, they eventually worked out how to gain full access to the network. It was getting late, and Xiao decided to issue a set of electronic instructions via Jensen's secure network to locate Tom Jackson and Jason Jones in London. Overnight, Jensen's third-party contacts would input the photos of the pair provided by Xiao and search for matches on the various airport and rail CCTV networks throughout London. Xiao knew from discussions with Luna that the process was relatively slow, and that results before early morning on Friday were unlikely.

*

The Colombian drug cartel's head of security, Pablo Barato, had remained in Rome and was back in mafia boss Matteo Ricci's office in Rome. Ricci's immediate superior, Alfonso Rossa was also in the room.

'I warned you not to make a permanent enemy of me when we met in this office two days ago.' Barato was an imposing figure even when seated. It was plain to see that he was furious.

'And we haven't,' Rossa was quick to respond, eyeballing his South American counterpart. Rossa had a similar physique to Matteo Ricci. The pair worked out together in the gym with heavy weights three times a week. Neither was as tall as the drug cartel's head of security, although each had an equally intimidating presence.

'I told you to deal with the Chinese pair, Ping Xiaoyan and Yen Chow Yu, and you haven't been able to. Another fail. You sent the same two enforcers who weren't up to the task here in Rome on Monday, and they were killed by Xiao and Yu. Fortunately for you, Yen Chow Yu was eliminated by a competent security operative protecting Jackson and his party.'

'Let's take a step back for a moment.' Alfonso Rossa was the consummate diplomat in situations such as this. He could also switch persona to ruthless mafia boss in a heartbeat.

Matteo Ricci agreed with his superior's approach to the problems at hand. Diplomacy was a far less disruptive way to achieve a meeting of the minds between two such powerful and violent groups.

'Yes, we have again underestimated Xiao and Yu, and we have lost two of our best enforcers in the process. Yu is dead, and we have yet to locate Xiao. We will, and we will eliminate her. We have in the meantime made good use of the information you provided on the likely whereabouts of Murray Jensen's tech expert, Luna Smythe. She was located in Nice yesterday and killed by lethal injection that simulates a heart attack. Under questioning before succumbing to her fatal heart attack, Smythe was able to tell us that she was indeed working with the Chinese pair, who we know at the time were in London.'

'Do you have a current lead on Xiao?' Barato was still glaring at the pair.

'Not yet. Jensen's jet returned to an airport near Nice this morning, and we have people on the ground trying to establish whether Xiao was on board, and if so where she may have gone.' Rossa spoke in an easy-going manner.

'I too have this information, and also have people on the ground searching for Xiao.' Barato's forearm muscles had grown taut.

'Then we must stay in touch and compare notes. We do, after all, want the same thing.' Rossa had stood first to signal that the meeting in his offices had ended.

Pablo Barato took the hint and stood to leave. He spoke before turning towards the door. 'I agree. We do both want the same thing. Let's stay in touch.'

After the South American had left, Matteo and Alfonso stayed in the room to strategise. They agreed it was important to be the ones to kill Ping Xiaoyan, but neither was averse to assistance from the drug cartel's people.

Chapter 32

DAY 12 (Friday)

Xaio was impatient to see the results of her overnight enquiries concerning Tom Jackson's whereabouts. She wasn't disappointed. The report was in. Tom Jackson had been identified in CCTV footage from the Bromley South overland railway station. The still photograph included with the report provided the confirmation Xiao needed to resume her search. Jackson was accompanied by the tall blonde security operative. The time stamp on the photograph was mid-afternoon on Thursday. Xiao knew that while she didn't yet have a location of the new safe house it was highly likely to be nearby to the CCTV sighting. She gave instructions to the pilot to return her to London that morning.

*

'I wish you and Willow hadn't left the safe house yesterday, Tom.' Jones had cautioned against the excursion.

'I needed to stretch my legs, and besides, we didn't go far. I had Willow with me, and we were shadowed by two of Oliver's highly trained operatives. Xiao is only one person, and as far as we understand it, the Sicilian mafia is still trying to track her down and eliminate her. We also have UK INTERPOL constantly scanning CCTV networks in and around London for her. For all

155

we know she has already departed for another country.' Jackson sounded a lot more confident and relaxed than he felt. 'I do agree, though, that we need to continue to exercise a high degree of care until she is located and captured or killed.'

'I would say an extreme level of caution is warranted until that bitch is neutralised once and for all.' Jones was flexing his fingers giving the impression that he remained in a battle-ready status.

'I have more work to get through this morning and over lunch. I'm contemplating another stroll around mid-afternoon through the external mall shopping area again. Would you like to join us?'

'Okay. But you know I don't like it, Tom. I'll get an update from Inspector Mason before we head out. Xiao is not someone we can afford to underestimate.' Jones was obviously concerned at Tom's cavalier attitude.

Jackson found it hard to function without some kind of regular exercise. A stroll through an external shopping mall accompanied by four highly trained security experts, and at a less busy time, was hardly an excessive risk.

*

The forensic team ordered by the French gendarmes had arrived at Luna Smythe's hotel the day before, not long after Xiao's theft of Smythe's laptop. The gendarmes on site could not immediately explain to the forensic specialists why the equipment was no longer in the locked hotel room.

Investigations overnight revealed a break-in at the rear of the hotel and the impersonation of a cleaner for a short time. Hidden security camera footage showed only a brief image of the intruder as they entered and exited the fire stairs on ground level. They had cleverly avoided all other security cameras. The intruder was clearly a woman although no facial image had been captured.

In talking with the forensic team during a follow-up visit, one of the gendarmes who had been stationed out the front of the hotel had mused aloud as to whether the small, fat Englishman with frayed ginger hair was in any way connected with the theft. He had occupied their attention asking about the equipment at about the same time as it was being stolen.

Without reaching any conclusion, a brief report was prepared for their records and forwarded to French INTERPOL, who for some reason had taken a particular interest in the case. That report was immediately shared with Italian INTERPOL.

A pair of enforcers from each of the Sicilian mafia and the South American drug cartel had remained in Nice overnight. Both were searching for the pilot of Murray Jensen's private jet, which they knew was currently in a private hangar at a small airport not far from Nice. If Xiao was not with him, the plan was to question him about her whereabouts. The two teams were not working together, although each was aware of the other's existence.

Information from Italian INTERPOL quickly filtered through to the mafia enforcers, via their Roman office. Matteo Ricci passed on the report along with confirmation that the gendarme's description of the short, portly British ginger matched the description of the pilot of Jensen's jet. The grainy silhouette of the hotel intruder, who was the likely thief of the laptop, matched the description of Ping Xiaoyan. Ricci said that the reason for the theft of the laptop was less significant than the confirmation that both the pilot and Xiao were together, and in Nice the day before.

The process was a little less circuitous, and the resulting information flow was the same, for the drug cartel enforcers. The cartel's local asset had managed to bribe the head of the investigating forensic team, who had shared his knowledge of the events that had unfolded at the hotel. The significance of the theft was more apparent to the drug cartel than to the mafia. Their security chief, Pablo Barato, was well aware that Luna Smythe had re-established Murray Jensen's entire secure global network while she and Jensen were their guests in the Ecuadorian Amazon jungle.

Access to Jensen's secure network and associated assets would make Xiao extremely dangerous. Barato had escalated the imperative to kill Xiao on sight and retrieve or destroy Smythe's laptop.

If that meant open cooperation with the Sicilian mafia, the drug cartel operatives were instructed to do just that.

The enforcer teams from the Sicilian mafia and the Colombian drug cartel arrived at the small airport outside Nice at almost the same time, only to find the hangar, where Jensen's private jet had been the day before, empty.

Chapter 33

Inspector Mason received the update report about events in Nice from the Italian INTERPOL. He had not initially been able to determine if the new information was significant or not, and decided to call and update Jason Jones.

'Morning, Inspector. Any news?' Jones was keen to find out where Xiao was.

'Nothing specific about the current location of Xiao. There has been a report from my colleagues at Italian INTERPOL about further events at the hotel in Nice where Luna Smythe's body was discovered yesterday.'

'Go ahead, mate. I'm all ears.' Jones smiled to himself, visualising Inspector Mason raising his bushy grey eyebrows in surprise at his familiarity and plain language. Jason activated speaker mode on his phone and signalled Tom and Willow to listen in.

'Yes, well.' Mason cleared his throat. 'The report in just now makes reference to a break-in yesterday at Smythe's hotel in Nice, and the theft of her laptop and associated hardware. A grainy security camera picture of the suspected thief matches the description of Ping Xiaoyan. A short, overweight British man with ginger hair was also reported chatting to the gendarmes outside the front of the hotel about Luna Smythe at around the time of the theft. He apparently said he worked for Smythe and was there to collect her personal belongings, including specifically the laptop. The British man ended the conversation abruptly and left. A distraction perhaps?'

'Interesting. Any insights?' Jones was scratching his unshaven stubble, deep in thought. He glanced at Tom and Willow, who both shrugged.

'Actually, yes. It's got me thinking, and I'm doing so on the run here. We know that Luna Smythe had been Murray Jensen's tech expert before going to work with Oliver Planksmith. We also know that Smythe had been on Jensen's payroll while working with Oliver. It was Smythe who freed herself and then masterminded a daring escape for Jensen while he was en-route to a maximum-security facility six months ago.'

'We're with you so far, Inspector.' Jackson entered the conversation, careful not to interrupt Inspector Mason's train of thought.

'Jensen and Smythe have both been out of action for six months and have resurfaced at around the same time. It's quite reasonable to assume that Smythe had continued to work for Jensen right up until his death in Rome last Sunday. My guess is she was working with him to re-establish his secure global communications network, which we dismantled in our raids on Jensen's London operations last year.'

'So you think Smythe's laptop may be the key to accessing Murray Jensen's global network?' Jason's thought process had caught up with the inspector's.

'Spot on, Jones. What's more interesting is that we know Xiao and Jensen were working together up until Jensen's death. It's not unreasonable to assume Xiao and Smythe continued to work together after Jensen was killed.' Mason sounded as if he was on a roll with his thought processes.

'So do you think Xiao killed Smythe and stole her laptop?' Willow was also thinking out loud.

'No. If Xiao had killed Smythe she would have taken the laptop straight away. I suspect Xiao was elsewhere when Smythe was killed and returned to steal the laptop after she heard of Smythe's demise.' Mason was making notes to record his own thought processes as he spoke.

'So who's the little fat Pommy ranga?' Jones heard the audible intake of air on the other end of the phone.

'Hmm. Good question.' Tom was impressed with Mason's restraint. He was clearly doing his best to ignore Jones' disrespectful humour. 'I might reach out to my Italian colleagues to see if they can shed any light on this. I'll do that now, and call you back.'

After the call with Mason ended, Tom, Jason and Willow sat down to discuss the significance of the new information. They did not get too far with their thought process before Inspector Mason called Jason's mobile.

Jones answered the call, activating speaker mode. 'That was quick, Inspector. You're again on speaker with Tom and Willow.'

'My Italian colleagues were able to tell me that the portly vertically challenged British fellow with the ginger hair is likely to be the pilot of Murray Jensen's private jet.' Mason's pause was no doubt so he could enjoy his listener's response to his attempt at wit.

Jason didn't disappoint. 'Good one, Willy. So you do have a sense of humour.' He had heard Inspector Darwin from Australian INTERPOL call Inspector Mason 'Willy' and those present, including Tom, and been amused at Mason's response.

'Anyway, moving along.' It was clear to Tom that Mason was not accustomed to Australian humour and was quickly regretting his attempt to reciprocate. 'They were also able to provide registration details of the jet. I'm not exactly sure how they came by this information, but I didn't ask. We've been able to trace the jet to a small airstrip just outside Nice, where it was hangered overnight. It flew out again this morning, destination unknown.'

'Jackson here, Inspector. Did your Italian colleagues have anything further to say about the laptop?'

'No unfortunately, although I think we can work that out for ourselves. If it truly is the key to accessing Murray Jensen's global network, and that is now in Xaio's hands, she will be a real force to be reckoned with.'

Jones jumped in. 'I agree. She could either be heading to some remote destination to lick her wounds and rebuild, or she could be on her way here to finish the job she and Yen Chow Yu were unable to complete in Rome on Monday and again here in London on Wednesday.'

'I share your opinions on this, Jones. Let's assume, at least until we know otherwise, that Xiao is on her way back to London today. She may even be here already. I'll continue to have my resources keep a watch for her.' Inspector Mason was about to end the call. 'One final thought. Since you moved to your current secure location in Bromley have any of you been out and about in areas that might be covered by London's comprehensive CCTV network?'

'Willow and I had a brief stroll around the Bromley Mall yesterday afternoon. I'm not sure about the whereabouts of the CCTV cameras you're thinking of. Why do you ask?' Jackson was curious.

'If you went anywhere near the Bromley South overland railway station, then it's possible your image was captured on the CCTV network. One thing we were able to establish from a forensic review of Murray Jensen's operations after our raids last year was that he had somehow been able to access the CCTV networks in and around London airports and train stations. It's a stretch I know, but if Xiao has access to Jensen's old network through Smythe's laptop, she could already have access to any relevant CCTV footage.'

'Okay, thanks, Inspector. As you say, it's a stretch. We don't even know if Xiao has been able to access anything at all through Smythe's laptop.' Jackson was dismissive of the unlikely possibility that Xiao already knew of their current whereabouts. But it didn't stop him from experiencing a cold chill as he thought about the prospect of rediscovery by her.

'We'll keep him under wraps, Mason,' Jones interjected. 'Let's just say that Tom and I have agreed to disagree on the current security risks. In the meantime, please get back to us as soon as you have any success with locating Xiao.'

'Will do. Take care all.' Inspector Mason ended the call.

Chapter 34

The two pairs of enforcers, one from the Sicilian mafia and the other from the Colombian drug cartel, had kept a wary eye on each other as they reported the empty hangar near Nice to their superiors.

'Matteo here. What's your report?'

'We've located the private hangar at the small airstrip outside Nice. It's empty.'

'Merda, shit! Anyone nearby who can shed any light on timing of departure?'

'Yes, boss. A nearby mechanic confirmed departure a little over thirty minutes ago. We had to ask him extra nicely for the likely destination. He said he heard the pilot and a Chinese woman talking about an airstrip north of London.'

'I'll send our jet to you, with instructions to head back to London. Stand by.' Matteo was about to end the call.

'One other thing, boss.'

'Wait one while I redirect our pilot.' After a brief pause, Matteo Ricci returned to the call. 'Our jet will be at your site in twenty minutes. What else?'

'It looks like our friends from the South American drug cartel are progressing their hunt for Xiao at the same pace as us. They're here.'

'No surprise there. Let me check for directions and get back to you.'

'Inteso, understood.'

Matteo Ricci ended the call and dialled his superior, Alfonso Rossa.

'Si, Matteo.'

'Ping Xiaoyan and the pilot have left Nice, headed for London. Our team has company at the now empty hangar just outside Nice. A pair of enforcers from the drug cartel. We knew they were on Xiao's trail and it's now obvious they have access to the same real time information as us.'

'As we discussed yesterday following our meeting with the cartel's head of security, Pablo Barato, it might be in our best interests to work alongside the cartel. It remains critical for us to be the ones to kill Xiao. I'll put you on hold and call Barato now to get his approval to join forces.'

Alfonso returned to his call with Matteo in less than two minutes. 'Barato is in agreement for the combination of our forces to hunt and kill Xiao. He doesn't care who kills the Chinese woman, as long as someone does. Curiously, he said that in exchange for letting our enforcers have first shot at Xiao, he wants us to hand over any laptop Xiao may have with her. When I asked him about this all he was prepared to do was confirm that it was the late Luna Smythe's laptop. He did say that if recovery of the laptop was in doubt then it must be destroyed. It all makes a little more sense now. My guess is the laptop provides a way into Murray Jensen's global network.'

'So what's your wish, boss?' Matteo was reasonably certain he knew what Alfonso Rossa would tell him to do.

'Kill the Chinese witch and destroy any laptop she is carrying. The last thing we need is for a South American drug cartel to exponentially expand its reach overnight. Don't make the destruction of the laptop too obvious, and if you have to kill the drug cartel enforcers to cover anything up, don't hold back.'

'Understood, boss.' Matteo allowed his boss to end the call, before dialling his team at the airport in Nice.

'Matteo here. This is what I want you to do.' Matteo spent the next few minutes explaining what was required of his enforcers. 'Questions?' There were none.

The mafia enforcers headed warily over to their drug cartel counterparts, weapons holstered and arms stretched out wide to their sides. The Columbian enforcers had just completed a call with their boss, Pablo Barato, and knew what to expect. In halting English, the group agreed they would travel together to London on the mafia's private jet to eliminate the Chinese woman Ping Xiaoyan. Not long afterwards, the jet arrived and the four large men boarded and took their seats. They were about one hour behind Xiao's flight.

*

By the time the mafia's jet was half way between Nice and London, Xiao's plane had touched down. She knew that the British authorities would be keeping a watch for her, and most likely also the recognisable pilot. She directed the pilot to stay with the jet and keep it ready for an immediate departure. It had been a simple task to access Jensen's network and issue an order for private secure transport from the airport north of London to Norman Park, Bromley. She sat in the backseat and kept her head low. The darkened windows would ensure that she avoided unwanted detection by the CCTV traffic camera network. Xiao was dropped off at the park about one kilometre south of the Bromley South train station, where Jackson had been spotted the day before. Xiao was usually very disciplined at controlling her emotions, and was conscious of her recent momentary lapses in control. She would need to be patient if she were to locate Tom Jackson and Jason Jones. Her pulse quickened as she exited the transport vehicle. She knew she was close to her targets, and to eliminating those who had taken so much from her. It was just her now.

The other jet from Nice landed at the same airport. It took no time for the occupants to locate Xiao's pilot and persuade him to divulge where Xiao was headed. He didn't know exactly where, only that her quarry's last sighting was near the Bromley South overland rail station late yesterday. The mafia and cartel's local colleagues had each sent a vehicle to meet the plane, and they wasted no time heading after Xiao in their separate vehicles.

*

'Time for a stroll.' Jackson was stretching his legs. He leaned forward to touch his toes and stretch his arms and back. 'Who would like to join me?'

'Are you sure about this?' Jones had tried without success to talk Jackson out of another outing.

'What could go wrong, particularly if you and Willow are with me?' Tom felt a little reckless, although the chances Xiao had located them, or was even in the country, were extremely low. A small part of him relished the prospect of luring Xiao out of hiding and seeing her eliminated once and for all.

'At least let me get an update from Inspector Mason.'

'You win, Jason, but make it quick please. I still have plenty of work to do.'

Jones dialled Inspector Mason, who confirmed there was nothing new to report. Jones told him that, against his better judgement, they were about to head out for a stroll around the outside shopping mall. Mason had promised to remain vigilant and to call or message Jones the moment he had new information.

'Nothing new to report, Tom. Let's go. Willow, you stay by Tom's side. I'll be a few paces behind. We'll take two of Oliver's security operatives with us to watch our flanks. Stay away from Bromley South and Bromley North train stations. Comms on, everyone.'

Chapter 35

Ping Xiaoyan walked the short distance from Norman Park to the Bromley South train station in less than twenty minutes. She kept Luna Smythe's laptop with her for several reasons. First and foremost, she didn't trust the pilot enough to leave the laptop with him. Xiao also needed the laptop to check on any updates from the ongoing CCTV monitoring she had initiated the day before, and to facilitate her extraction and return to the private jet.

To others, it may seem like a wild goose chase to take up a position from which to observe the Bromley South train station and wait. She was a keen study of human nature and knew that many were creatures of habit. She was hoping that Tom Jackson would choose to have an afternoon walk in the same vicinity, reasoning that he would not wish to stray too far from his new safe house.

By arrangement made on the flight from Nice, the mafia enforcers were dropped off at the Bromley North train station and the drug cartel enforcers were taken to Bromley South. They each arrived at around the same time, almost an hour after Xiao had taken up her position at a window seat inside Café Nero opposite the Bromley South train station. Each pair of enforcers knew what was required of them, although the instructions to the mafia enforcers with respect to Smythe's laptop were markedly different. Cooperation between the two sets of enforcers had seemed like a good idea to their respective superiors, and in the main it was. Two distinct disadvantages were, however, very apparent to those in the field. There was a severe language barrier, and, more importantly, no means of effective communication during the operation.

Xiao saw the two burly South Americans exit the vehicle in the drop-off area adjacent to the train station. She was instantly on the alert, although she did not recognise either of them. Their presence could be completely unrelated to hers. Her instincts told her otherwise. The men immediately split up and took up separate positions from which to observe the train station. Xiao could see the telltale bulges in their jackets indicating each was carrying a weapon in a shoulder holster. Interesting. Xiao had no way of knowing if the pair was there for her, Jackson, Jones, all three, or none of them.

At the northern end of the shopping mall, the mafia pair had decided to stay together, in plain sight. They set off walking at a slow tourist-like pace down the mall, heading for Bromley South train station. They were of the view that it was best to keep moving and blend in with the rest of the crowd. One of the pair nudged his colleague as soon as he spotted Tom Jackson and Willow Douglas. The colleague acknowledged the sighting and they both continued down the mall away from Jackson, heading for their South American counterparts.

*

Jones managed to persuade Tom to take a different route to the shopping mall. One that ensured they stayed well away from any train station CCTV cameras.

'Cracker day, Tom, Willow and gentlemen.' Jason was testing the comms he shared with Jackson, Willow and the two Planksmith operatives guarding their flanks. The responses were immediate and mostly professional.

'One, copy.'

'Two, copy.'

'Agreed. Think I'll head to that German sausage stall today. My mouth watered for a long time after I passed it yesterday. I owe it to my stomach to ingest one today.' Tom was smiling at Willow, who laughed and called in, 'Three, copy.'

'One here. I saw a pair of European gentlemen pass by a short time ago. They may simply be tourists, although they looked a little out of place. They continued in a southerly direction. I'll keep an eye out for them. Both tall with weight-lifter physiques and wearing cheap-looking tweed coats. Both have salt and pepper hair slicked back in the typical style for middle-aged European men.'

'Roger that. Break off and follow at a safe distance. Report anything unusual,' Jones said quietly.

Tom glanced at Willow, who shrugged and winked. 'Let's go and get your sausage.' She mouthed the words so that the others would not hear them over the comms.

Jackson smiled broadly.

*

Xiao had waited patiently, comfortable in the knowledge that she had a clear line of sight to both of the burly South Americans. She had just checked again for any updated sightings of Jackson or Jones on the CCTV network sweep, which had continued to run its delayed analysis. Negative.

Xiao sat up in her café chair when she observed a large Italian-looking man in a cheap tweed jacket with slicked-back hair approach one of the burly pair. They conversed briefly before the Italian left, retracing his steps in a northerly direction. The man who had been spoken to crossed the road to confer with his colleague. They left almost immediately, heading away separately, both in a northerly direction.

Xiao told herself this could be it. It made sense to her that both the Italian mafia and the Colombian drug cartel would send enforcers to apprehend or eliminate her. She packed the laptop into the carry case, involuntarily holding it tighter than she needed, and left the café to head in a northerly direction.

In her haste to follow the three enforcers, Xiao had momentarily forgotten the position of the CCTV cameras at the Bromley South train station. Unlike her delayed reporting from the sweep of the CCTV camera network, INTERPOL's was immediate.

'Got a hit, sir,' one of Inspector Mason's task force allocated to hunting and capturing Xiao called out, his hand above his head. 'Up on screen one.'

Inspector Mason looked up at screen number one to see the unmistakable figure of Ping Xiaoyan, and immediately reached for his mobile phone. Mason decided it would be more efficient to message Jones with the information rather than call him. He could then relay it to his security team.

Jones felt his phone vibrate in his pocket and removed it to see Mason's message: **Ping Xiaoyan spotted at the Bromley South train station. Last seen heading north.**

'Heads up, all,' Jones said into the shared comms. 'Mason tells me that Chinese bitch has been spotted leaving the Bromley South train station and is headed our way.'

'One here. The European pair split up briefly. One of them conferred with a burly South American-looking gentleman, who crossed the road to speak to another with a similar heritage. Both are wearing tracksuits and joggers. One black and the other navy blue. The Europeans are back together and heading north, followed closely by the South Americans who have again separated.'

'Copy that. Fuck! Looks like we have a pair of mafia enforcers and a pair of drug cartel enforcers converging on our position. Xiao is also headed our way. Try and avoid killing the Italians in the tweed jackets unless they pose a threat. Treat the drug cartel in the tracksuits the same way but with a much lower level of tolerance. No telling why those pricks are here.' Jones was in control. He lived for these moments and felt his adrenaline surge as his concern for Jackson's safety escalated.

Chapter 36

Jackson had selected the spicy smoked German sausage with a sweet chilli sauce. Willow had done the same. She said she wasn't hungry but had whispered to Tom that she wanted to enjoy the same sausage experience.

Tom had taken his first bite of the gourmet German hot dog when he heard Jason's warning.

Willow took charge. 'We're too exposed where we are, Jason.'

'Agreed. Head for the nearby Pret A Manger shop and hide in the back section. There should be a rear exit. Check and confirm.' Jones had spotted the nearby ready-made sandwich and breakfast chain shop and registered it as contingency cover in his mind as soon as Tom and Willow had stopped at the German sausage stall.

'Copy that. On our way.' Willow had grabbed Tom's arm and was directing him towards the near empty Pret A Manger shop.

Jackson knew he was well protected. It was critical that he obeyed directions without question or hesitation. His analytical mind was working overtime. He tallied the numbers. His protective force was four strong. Xiao was on her own, and hell-bent on revenge against he and Jason. The Italian pair was possibly there to protect him from Xiao, and was definitely there to kill Xiao. Who knew why the South American pair were there, although it did sound like they were communicating with the Italians. Jackson

172

thought it was best to assume it was five of us, including himself, against five of them.

Jackson was drawn back to the present. He and Willow were making their way to the rear of the sandwich shop when he heard Jones again.

'Willow, is there a back exit?'

'Affirmative. Leads to a back laneway heading in both directions.' Willow had opened the rear door, ignoring protests from the shop manager. The manager reached for her mobile phone, no doubt to dial the police on 999. Willow discouraged her from doing so by displaying her now drawn Glock handgun. 'We're the good guys,' Willow whispered, her finger to her lips. 'Sit there and stay quiet. We'll get the coppers after we deal with the assassin hunting us.' The manager did as she was told, cowering in the corner.

'Two, circle around to that rear laneway and provide backup for an extraction. Willow, open the rear door when two knocks twice.'

'Two, copy.'

'Three, copy.' Jackson knew that Willow was a highly trained professional like her colleagues. He could nevertheless still see the concern registered on her face.

'One, do you have eyes on?' Jones again.

'One here. I have taken up a position on the other side of the mall from Pret A Manger. The Italian pair in the tweed jackets are together, and heading our way. I see one of the South Americans in the black tracksuit not far behind them, but have not sighted his colleague in the navy tracksuit. No sign of Xiao.'

'Copy that,' Jones responded. 'I'm on the other side of the mall from you, just south of the entrance to the sandwich shop. I see the bogey in the navy tracksuit on my side. Wait one. He's down. Fuck! Xiao came from nowhere and stuck him in the neck with an icepick. Went down like a bag of shit. She's just vanished like some kind of wraith.'

'One here. No reaction from the Italians or the remaining South American. They might be working together, but they do not have comms.'

'Roger that. Willow, hold firm. Xiao is on the scene.'

'Three, copy.'

Jackson could hear all of the communications, and it surprised him how relatively calm he was. He was not trained for this, but he had been here before. Maybe this was the beginning of the end of the evil that had haunted him for the last two years.

The Colombians did not have any form of sophisticated comms. They had, however, maintained line of sight of each other. The drug cartel enforcer in the black tracksuit had seen his colleague in the navy tracksuit on the other side of the mall go down and darted over to assist. Xiao had lain in wait. As soon as the new arrival had bent down to check his colleague's pulse, Xiao rendered him the same fate.

Bystanders were starting to react to the two fallen men and the sight of the spreading pools of life-blood. Some were screaming. Others were dialling 999.

'Holy shit,' Jones shouted into his comms. 'The other guy in the black tracksuit has just suffered the same fate as his colleague. Both down and out. That fucking hell-bitch came out of nowhere, and she's disappeared again. Blood everywhere. People are starting to react. The police will be all over this place shortly. Willow, I'm heading your way to assist with extraction. One, maintain cover from your side.'

'Three, copy.' Willow turned her attention to Tom. 'Ready?' Jackson nodded.

'One, copy.'

'Russell, you nearby?' Jones was signalling their ever-present driver tasked by Oliver Planksmith to shadow Jackson and his party.

'Affirmative. Out back of Pret A Manger with two. Your call on extraction.'

'Roger that.'

*

'Got you.' Xiao had spotted Jason Jones break cover and head for the Pret A Manger shop. With surprising speed, she quickly covered the distance between her and Jones. She reached for the ceramic icepick in her boot and was about to plunge it into Jason's neck when she was bowled over by a figure charging from the entrance to the sandwich shop. Her initial surprise was replaced by a feeling of elation as she sprang to her feet like a coiled spring, realising that her assailant was Tom Jackson. She rounded on Jackson, relishing the thought of eliminating both of her arch-enemies in the one battle. She was not expecting neither Jackson nor Jones to be a match for her. She lunged at Jackson with the icepick, certain in the knowledge that the razor-sharp weapon would draw his full attention, allowing her to land a disabling kick to his kidneys. Underestimating Jackson was a mistake. He countered her move with his own ferocious kick, deflecting her airborne leg. As she fell back, a shot rang out from the other side of the mall.

*

'I just winged Xiao. Right shoulder.' One was on the move.

Jones had seen Jackson speed past him and heard the thud as he collided with Xiao. He spun around to see a mix of rage and pain in Xiao's eyes. She was unbalanced from the gunshot to her shoulder. He kicked her legs out from under her, and she regained her feet almost as if she had landed on a trampoline. Jones could see the Italian pair converging from the other side of the mall, guns drawn.

'New threat. Italians headed our way, weapons hot.' The timeline for Jones slowed. He saw that Willow had arrived and dragged Tom back to the safety of the shop. Jones studied the injured Xiao, who was circling him, frothing at the mouth like a rabid dog. He reminded himself that he had seen that exact same look before on the face of the now deceased leader of the criminal syndicate, Adrian Low. It also occurred to him that Xiao used an icepick in the same manner, and with the same lethal effect, as the deceased syndicate assassin, Madeline Peel. Surely not. Could all these evil fuckers be related?

Jones had no way of knowing if the Italians meant him any harm. He knew with certainty that they planned to kill Xiao. He turned and raced into the sandwich shop not far behind Tom and Willow.

'One. Do you have a clear line of sight to Xiao.'

'Negative.'

'Leave the Chinese bitch to the mercy of the Italians. Kill her if they can't. Don't harm them unless they move to follow me. Extraction paramount. You're on your own for now. No unnecessary risks. I'll send two your way.'

'One, copy.'

Jones raced through to the back of the Pret A Manger shop, past the sobbing manager, and out into the alleyway. He directed two to return and assist one, and followed Tom and Willow into the car. Russell sped away, headed for the safe house.

'What the fuck was that, Tom?' Jones was fully aware that Tom's instincts had saved him from a certain violent death.

'You're welcome.'

*

Xiao heard the footsteps behind her and turned to see the advancing Italians, guns drawn. Out of the corner of her eye, she saw Jones disappear into the sandwich shop. In the blink of an eye, she drew her gun from the small of her back with her left hand and fired it at the nearest Italian, shooting him between the eyes. Xiao reasoned that her reprieve was likely caused by the Italians not wanting to fire their guns while Jones was in their line of fire. *Weak*, she thought as she switched her aim to the other Italian. It was her last thought. The remaining Italian had not been distracted by his fallen colleague and had fired as soon as Jason Jones was out of the line of fire. He shot Xiao through the right eye. Another shot through the left eye while she was on the ground not only ensured her fate, but it left a clear message to all that she had been assassinated by the Sicilian mafia.

'One here. Xiao is down and out. One Italian remaining. No apparent threat. Instructions?'

'This is Jones. Confirm Xiao is deceased.'

'Confirmed.'

Jones was punching the air, and Tom and Willow embraced in the back seat. 'Can you retrieve the laptop?'

'Two here. Negative. The large Italian man is smashing it to pieces and shooting the shit out of the hard drives. His other hand is signalling us to back off.'

'Stand down and allow him to leave. Exit the way we left, and pronto. I can hear whistles and sirens everywhere. The place will be crawling with coppers and emergency vehicles within minutes. Rendezvous back at the safe house.'

'One, copy.'

'Two, copy.'

'Ding dong! The witch is dead.' Jones was mirroring Russell's wide grin.

Chapter 37

Jones was on the phone to Inspector Mason before their car travelled the relatively short distance to the nearby safe house. Russell had intentionally chosen a circuitous route.

'Mason, you need to get your people on site at Bromley shopping mall. There are dead bodies everywhere, and police and emergency vehicles are arriving en masse.'

'I'm seeing the secure information feeds from the area. Looks like a war zone. Is everyone on our side safe?' Mason was viewing live feed from surrounding CCTV cameras on three separate wall-mounted screens in his situation room.

'Affirmative. Xiao is down for the count, as are two South American drug cartel enforcers and one Sicilian mafia enforcer. How soon can you be on site?' Jones was thinking ahead to next steps.

'I'll secure the area now and should be able to get there within the hour.'

'Good, I'll meet you on site and take you through the events as they took place before bodies are cleared away.'

'Very helpful, thanks Jones. See you on site shortly.' Inspector Mason disconnected the call and set about contacting his law enforcement counterparts to let them know the kill zone was under INTERPOL control. Nothing was to be touched until he was on site. The public were to be kept well away.

Jason, Tom and Willow exited the car and entered the safe house from the rear.

'Mason will cordon off the site for he and I to do a walk through before bodies can be removed. He'll be on site within the hour. I'll head back shortly and wait for him. I'd say the threat has been averted. It's hard to see any remaining threat, but let's just take a cautious approach for now,' Jones spoke quickly. His adrenaline levels remained elevated.

Jackson looked down at the gourmet German hot dog he was clutching tightly in his hand. 'Huh! I've still got hold of this. Lucky I didn't have to fight my way out of there. I might have had to waste it. I only managed to have one bite before the shitfight. I don't think I'll return to the scene with you, Jason. I'll stay here with Willow and finish what we started at the German sausage stall.'

'That's hilarious, Tom. You must be very fond of those things. I ditched mine the moment Jason warned us of the approaching danger.' Willow was smiling broadly with relief.

'What can I say. I love my sausage.' Jackson's smile mirrored Willow's.

'Oh dear. Keep this up and you two might need to get a room.' Jones was laughing and peering out the window as Tom and Willow shared a knowing look. 'I'll head over to make sure the coppers have the 'hands-off' message from Inspector Mason. One, come with me, just in case that mafia fucker's instructions have changed.'

'Copy that.'

'The rest of you stay here and make sure Tom stays the fuck inside for now.'

Willow Douglas nodded, and the remaining two Planksmith operatives acknowledged the instructions.

*

The surviving mafia enforcer was long gone. He left the scene immediately after he had killed Xiao and destroyed the laptop. He kept the internal hard drive from the laptop to prove it had been damaged beyond repair. He was travelling in the same vehicle he had arrived in and was approaching the airport where the mafia's jet was parked.

'It's Georgio, boss.' He had waited until he was well clear of ground zero before calling Matteo Ricci.

'I'm getting news reports of a suspected terrorist attack in Bromley in London. What the fuck is going on over there?' Ricci had been anxious to hear from his enforcers and had been loath to call during an operation.

'Xiao killed our colleague. Shot him between the eyes. She also killed both Colombians. Icepick to the carotid artery. Very quick. I repaid the favour, with extreme prejudice.'

'Xiao is dead, and you killed her?' It was music to Matteo's ears.

'Si. I shot her in both eyes. Our calling card.'

'Molto bene, very good. And the laptop?'

'Destroyed. I shot up the hard drives, and brought the one from inside the smashed-up laptop with me to prove it.'

'Well done. Sorry about our colleague. I will let his next of kin know. That's the third one we've lost to the Chinese bitch. At least she's finally out of the picture. What about Jensen's pilot?'

'I've just arrived at the airport. I'll see if I can locate him.' Georgio paused his call with Ricci while he searched for the pilot. 'No sign of him, boss. The jet is locked down. Shall I look for him?'

'No, he's harmless. Return home. I'll report up the line and they can tell the drug cartel people what went down.'

*

Jones was joined on site by Inspector Mason and a forensic team from INTERPOL. The local police had cordoned off the area and kept the public well away, waiting for Mason to arrive. Only one person had required medical attention. The manager of the Pret A Manger store was being treated for severe shock.

'Mason.' Jones held out his hand.

'Jones.' Mason took the proffered hand and winced as his pudgy hand was squeezed tightly by Jones, without thinking.

'Sorry.' Jones released his grip and withdrew his hand. 'Still in fight-or-flight mode, I think.'

'No problem, Jones. I understand.' Mason was shaking his hand slightly, causing his jowls to wobble. 'Now, tell me what went down here. I can see four bodies.'

Jones described the events that took place after he, Jackson and their protective unit had left the safe house for a walk.

'We were already on alert when you messaged that Xiao had been identified. Our guys had spotted the Italian enforcers. It all happened pretty quickly after that. We think the gents in the tracksuits over there are South American drug cartel enforcers. They were dispatched clinically by Xiao. Icepick to the neck. I still don't know if they were here for us, or working with the Italians to kill Xiao. It appeared that the Italians and the South Americans were communicating, so they may not have been a threat to us. I guess we'll never know for sure. Xiao had been winged in the shoulder by one of Oliver's team from the other side of the mall. The Italian over there with the bullet between his eyes was running in my direction to kill Xiao before she could do me in. My guess is that I was in his line of fire so he couldn't shoot Xiao. As soon as I was out of the way the other Italian took her down with a shot through her eye. The shot through her other eye seems to be a little more symbolic.'

'Mafia calling card,' Mason said.

'That makes sense. The message to all is that the mafia killed Xiao. Perhaps that was for the benefit of the drug cartel people? Again, we'll never know for sure.'

'And the laptop.' Mason was pointing at the numerous pieces of the laptop and external hard drives that had been repeatedly stomped on and shot at.

'My guys say the Italian was quite passionate about it. He held them at bay while he did so. When he was done, he collected the mangled hard drive from inside the laptop and took it with him.'

Jones had started to relax a little as he neared the end of his story for Inspector Mason.

*

Murray Jensen's pilot, David, had seen his cushy lifestyle begin to evaporate. Jensen's violent death the preceding weekend in Rome and the killing of Luna Smythe this week in Nice were difficult for him to process. He had been left to the mercy of the ruthless Chinese woman, Ping Xiaoyan. She had directed him to stay with the jet at the airport north of London. He had been too anxious to do that and had followed Xiao to Bromley.

Contrary to what Xiao thought might be the case, UK IN-TERPOL did not have any alerts out for him. He didn't know for sure, but thought that might be the case. No one in his entire life had ever taken him as a serious threat. He was angry now that everything he had known for some time was being taken away from him. The pilot wasn't sure himself if he had followed Xiao to witness her death, or to see her triumph. He even thought he might take matters into his own hands if the opportunity presented itself, and free himself from her control.

The pilot had positioned himself a safe distance from Xiao, who had been too focused on her mission to notice him. He had seen everything unfold in front of him. As Xiao was finished off by the mafia enforcer, he knew his life had changed forever. He had nothing left. Maybe he could achieve what Xiao and her offsider, Yen Chow Yu, had not been able to.

*

Jones had finished relaying his story to Inspector Mason when he caught movement out of the corner of his eye. He turned to see a small rotund man with a comb-over heading quickly in his direction. His orange hair was wispy thin. The policewoman guarding that part of the cordoned off area was looking the other way.

Realisation dawned on Jones. The pilot. What could he possibly want. As Jones was trying to make sense of the situation, the pilot stretched his right arm in front of him. A spring-loaded mechanism in his sleeve delivered a snub-nose revolver into his hand.

'Gun,' Jones shouted as a shot rang out. His initial thought was that for a small gun it sure did make a big noise. At the same time, he felt the bullet thump into his flesh. Jones stumbled backwards, clutching the wound in his right side, just below his ribcage. He could instantly feel the warm flow of blood running down his side. His training kicked in and, ignoring his pain, he lunged towards the little fat man, dodging to the left as he did so. Another shot rang out. This one missed. Before the pilot could fire another shot, Jones bowled him over. The gun fell to the ground with a clatter as Jones rained blow after blow on the pudgy figure pinned underneath him.

'I've got this.' One placed his hand on Jason's shoulder, causing him to cease his blows.

Jones looked up to see his colleague pointing a gun at the bloody face of the unconscious figure of the pilot.

Chapter 38

Jones was sedated and taken to the nearby Princess Royal University Hospital in one of the many waiting ambulances. His gunshot wound was serious but not life threatening. None of his major organs had been damaged. The surgeon on duty in the Emergency Department thought it best to place Jason into an induced coma overnight, to allow his body to recover from the shock.

Tom and Willow had been left alone inside the safe house the prior evening after Jones had returned to the crime scene to meet up with Inspector Mason.

Jackson's phone rang. 'It's Inspector Mason. I need to get this. What! Is he okay? Which hospital? I'll meet you there shortly.'

'Jason's been shot by Jensen's pilot, who no one had thought to check on. He's been placed in a coma overnight. The surgeon thinks he's going to be okay, but only time will tell.'

They headed to the hospital, Jackson concerned for his good friend and protector.

Jones looked so uncharacteristically helpless lying there in the hospital bed, hooked up to all manner of breathing and other equipment. Tom stayed the night in a chair in the hospital room. The surgeon told him Jones would likely remain in the induced coma for up to twelve hours. Tom had remained, wanting to be there in case he woke up. Willow waited with him and arranged

184

for another Planksmith security operative to relocate to the exterior of the hospital.

Inspector Mason left the hospital soon after Tom and Willow arrived. He'd said he wanted to head back to the scene to make sure his forensic team had things under control. He also wanted to question the pilot.

Jones woke a little after eight a.m. Tom and Willow had managed to source a passable cappuccino for themselves at the hospital cafeteria, and were quietly chatting as they sipped from their disposable coffee cups.

'Did you get one for me?' Jones said weakly.

'Welcome back to the land of the living! I'll grab you one shortly, mate. How're you feeling?' Jackson went to hug him before reminding himself that Jones had been seriously wounded.

'Sore but fine. I can't believe that little fat ranga got me. I let my guard down and did not immediately see him as a threat.' Jones looked crestfallen.

'Don't be too hard on yourself, Jase. From what I heard, you reacted like a wounded wild animal and launched at the pilot, dodged the next shot, and immobilised him very quickly. You must've been pissed off because you had to be prevented from continuing to beat the man to a pulp, even after he was rendered unconscious.' Jackson moved his seat closer to the hospital bed.

'The pilot's injuries were not serious.' Tom and Willow turned to see Inspector Mason standing in the doorway to the room. 'Glad to see you're awake, Jones. I've just spoken to the surgeon, and he says you'll be fine after a few weeks' rest. He'll tell you himself, I'm sure, but you need to go easy on your stitches. There are plenty of them at the site of the bullet's entrance and exit points. He says you're quite fortunate the bullet passed through without damaging any major organs.'

'So the pilot's okay?' Jones was trying to sit up a little. Tom helped him relocate the support pillows behind him.

'Yes, just a little bruised and bloody. He has a broken nose, and possibly a fractured eye socket. He'll undergo X-rays in the prison hospital this morning. I did manage to have a brief chat with him this morning.' Mason brought another seat in from outside the room and lowered his bulk slowly into it.

'And what did the fat fuck have to say for himself.' Jones was recovering some of the volume to his voice.

Mason didn't react as Tom expected him to. Perhaps he had become accustomed to Jason's obscene language, or perhaps he was just making concessions because of Jason's situation. 'He confirmed our suspicions that the destroyed laptop was the one stolen from Luna Smythe's hotel room, and that it did indeed provide a window to Murray Jensen's global network. My guess is the drug cartel insisted it be delivered to them, and that the mafia decided they would rather see it destroyed than in the cartel's hands.'

'That makes sense. Anything else of interest?' Jackson asked.

'Actually, yes. Jason, you theorised to me yesterday that the late syndicate leader Adrian Low and Ping Xiaoyan could be related because of their distinctly similar reactions and facial features when injured and facing imminent capture. You also thought Xiao could be related to the infamous syndicate assassin Madeline Peel because of the near-identical lethal manner in which she wielded a ceramic icepick that she too kept concealed in her boot.' Mason could not contain his grin.

'And?' Jones was slumping back in his bed with exhaustion.

'You were spot on. Madeline Peel and Ping Xiaoyan were sisters. And here's the real kicker. Adrian Low was their father.'

'You're shitting me. That means Low killed his own daughter.' Tom could not believe what he was hearing.

'Exactly,' Mason continued. 'The world is better off without those lowlifes who will clearly stop at nothing to achieve their ends. Let's hope that the death of the two known remaining members of the Hong Kong-based syndicate and the death of Murray Jensen will see their respective operations unravel.

'The pilot directed us to Jensen's jet at an airport north of London, and it has been impounded. Another jet, believed to belong to the Sicilian mafia, was seen leaving the same airport late yesterday with one passenger. An onsite mechanic confirmed that the jet had arrived earlier in the day with four large male passengers.

'Not much we can do at this stage about the Sicilian mafia or the Colombian drug cartel. They look to have retreated to fight another day. Only time will tell.'

'So what's next, gentlemen?' Willow Douglas had been listening intently.

'I for one need some shuteye. Piss off the lot of you so I can rest.' Jones offered a tired smile and managed to wave his hand dismissively.

Jackson laughed. 'Sounds like the Jason I know. Rest up, buddy, and I'll check in on you later. I have plenty of work to do over the weekend on the back-up deal for the sale of the Italian theme park.'

'And I have plenty of paperwork and some further interrogation of the pilot. I'm hoping he can shed some light on whether or not there are any viable surviving remnants of either Murray Jensen's operation or the Hong Kong-based syndicate.' The inspector was levering himself out of the hospital chair as he spoke.

'One, this is three. We're about to leave the hospital and head back to the safe house. Remain on site and check on our patient from time to time. I'll leave a set of comms with him.' Willow had seamlessly reverted to her professional persona.

'Copy that.'

Chapter 39

The surviving mafia enforcer was in Matteo Ricci's office in Rome. Ricci's superior, Alfonso Rossa was also in the small room, as was the head of security for the drug cartel, Pablo Barato.

'Tell me again how Xiao was killed, and what happened to the laptop.' Barato remained standing, no doubt in an attempt to demonstrate he was in control of the meeting. Matteo knew that he and Alfonso would no longer allow the South American to intimidate them. He was, after all, on their home turf.

'Xiao was shot multiple times. She had been carrying the laptop in a shoulder bag and it got shot up in the process.' The mafia enforcer was shrugging his shoulders and holding his upturned hands in front of him.

'I don't believe you.' Barato clenched his large hands into fists and placed them on his hips.

'I'll prove it to you. See.' The enforcer produced the mangled internal hard drive from the laptop.

Ricci knew it was a mistake as soon as he sighted the hard drive. It was squashed and had multiple bullet holes in it. Why hadn't he checked it before the Colombian had arrived.

'What is this? It looks like it has been stomped on and intentionally shot multiple times at close range. I am told Xiao was shot three times. Once in the shoulder and once in each eye.' Barato was fuming.

'Didn't you tell me that once you were certain Xiao was down and out, you saw that the laptop was damaged beyond repair and wanted to be certain that no workable parts from it would fall into the hands of the authorities?' Matteo spoke evenly to his enforcer, while maintaining strong eye contact with the Colombian.

'Si. That is what I told you. There was much confusion and not a lot of time to think. I had to escape, but did not want to leave any part of the laptop for the authorities. I stomped and fired my pistol, grabbed the internal hard drive and ran.'

'I'm not convinced.' Barato turned to leave the meeting. 'One final thing. How was it that Xiao was able to access Smythe's computer?'

'I've been thinking about that myself.' Alfonso was on his feet. 'We do know that Xiao's financial knowledge and technical skills were second to none in her syndicate. We also suspect that she and Smythe enjoyed a close relationship. Perhaps Smythe shared log in details with her, or maybe she worked out a way to hack into the system through the laptop.'

'What about the pilot?' Barato stood in the doorway facing the group.

'The pilot?' Alfonso Rossa squinted his eyes and tilted his head.

'Jensen's pilot. He was with Jensen for a long time. He was also with Jensen and Smythe during much of their stay with us in Ecuador. Maybe he overheard enough to be able to access the laptop.'

'Good point. Hadn't thought of that.' Matteo Ricci was also now standing. 'The pilot was not at the airport near London and Jensen's plane was locked down.' Ricci looked to his enforcer who nodded his confirmation.

'Even if he doesn't know his way into Jensen's global network, he certainly knows too much about our respective operations. I plan to track him down and either encourage him to join our organisation or eliminate him.' Barato turned to leave.

'Before you leave.' Alfonso Rossa moved towards the door. 'Allow us to track the pilot down for you. We have no need for a pilot or another private jet. If he has no interest in joining you, we will finish him.' He held out his hand and Pablo Barato accepted it.

'You have forty-eight hours, and make sure no one else is harmed.' Barato turned and left the room.

'Fuck. The pilot! Why didn't we think of the risk he poses to all of us?' Alfonso was pacing back and forth in the small room, causing Matteo and the enforcer to resume their seats.

'Interesting isn't it how some people who are small in stature can sometimes fly under the radar.' Matteo ignored his own pun. This was a serious matter.

'We did see a news report that Jason Jones was shot by an unknown assailant sometime after the main events in Bromley were over and the authorities were on the scene. It didn't make sense at the time, but what if that was the pilot? I heard the assailant was seriously injured in the process.' Alfonso had stopped pacing.

'On it, boss. Leave it with me.' Matteo showed Alfonso to the door and returned to strategise with his enforcer.

*

The X-rays in the prison hospital confirmed that the pilot had suffered a fractured eye socket. His face had been cleaned and bandaged and he was sitting up in his hospital bed, sipping water through a straw, when Inspector Mason arrived to question him.

'You're rather lucky Jones was prevented from ending your life after you shot him.'

'I don't feel lucky.'

'Maybe you will be.' Mason lowered himself into yet another uncomfortable hospital chair.

'How so?'

'Well, that depends on what you know and whether you're prepared to cooperate with us.'

'I know a lot, and have nothing to lose by cooperating, except of course my life.'

'Maybe we could put you in a witness protection program and exempt you from prosecution.'

'Exempt from all prosecution, including my attempt to kill Jason Jones?'

'That depends on what you know and how it helps us. For starters, do you know if there are any remaining key players in either Murray Jensen's operations or the Hong Kong-based syndicate?'

'I'll answer that question now provided you agree to document your offer of witness protection and absolution from prosecution. I will also need one million American dollars.'

'I agree to present my written offer to you later today. Witness protection and absolution from prosecution should not be an issue. I'm not sure about the funding. There will be some, although perhaps not that much.'

'Okay, then. I am certain that without Jensen, Smythe or Xiao, Jensen's organisation will fragment and dissolve. That is unless someone is able to relatively quickly reactivate the secure network that Smythe had rebuilt for Jensen in South America.'

'And you know how to?' Mason was intrigued.

'I believe so, with a little technical assistance that I am sure you will have available.'

'Anybody else?'

'No. Jensen was paranoid about protecting the access protocols.'

'And the Hong Kong-based syndicate?'

'I am certain it ended with the deaths of Yen Chow Yu and Ping Xiaoyan. They were both control freaks and to my knowledge had not yet allowed anybody else into their inner circle.' The pilot had a smug look on his face.

'So what else do you know that you think might justify the deal you are after?'

'Ah, I was wondering when you'd get to that. I've given you all I am prepared to at the moment. What I can say is that I am an information gatherer. I have been with Murray Jensen for a long time and have learnt the power of information. I can tell you a significant amount about current operations of the Colombian drug cartel in the Amazon jungle east of Quito. One of the very few advantages I have experienced of being short and a little overweight is that no one seems to take me seriously. To many I am invisible. I am constantly surprised at the extent of confidential information I overhear. I know a lot about the drug cartel. Not as much, but still plenty, about the Sicilian mafia.'

Inspector Mason lifted himself slowly out of his chair. 'Very well then. I will be back later today with the paperwork.' Mason checked that the pilot was securely handcuffed to his hospital bed, and left after speaking with the prison guard outside the room.

Chapter 40

Jackson spent most of the day working with his Italian colleague Lorenzo Bassutri. To make amends for disclosing Tom's whereabouts to his family member in the Sicilian mafia earlier in the week, Lorenzo had worked tirelessly on the deal since.

The non-binding Terms Sheet had been signed the previous Thursday. With considerable assistance from Lorenzo, the primary documents were close to being finalised.

'There are only a few remaining issues for me to resolve with my client. Thank you, Lorenzo, for keeping the ball rolling on the document negotiation. I have been somewhat distracted over the last couple of days.'

'Si, Signor Tom. It was the least I could do for you after betraying your confidence. As I said at the time, I meant well, and I was not presented with any kind of choice.'

'I understand, Lorenzo.' Jackson did not, but wanted to be careful not to let those events impact on his client's commercial imperatives.

'I have seen only what the news stations have broadcast about yesterday's events. The police are remaining very tight-lipped about the detail. I hear Signor Jones may have been injured. I hope he's okay.'

'There's not a lot I can tell you at the moment, sorry Lorenzo. The police have asked us not to speak to anyone about the events while an active investigation remains underway. Let's just focus on the deal for now.' Tom did not trust Lorenzo's familial connection to the mafia.

'I completely understand that I have undermined your trust in me. If and when you are able to tell me more, I will be a willing listener. For now, I agree. Let's get on with the deal.'

'The way things are shaping up, we should be able to sign primary documents on Monday or Tuesday London time, and work towards completion by Friday.'

'Si. I agree. I have had a team working with me full time to satisfy the significant number of enquiries from the buyer's London lawyers. My team is in the office again with me today. The theme park is a complex asset with a multitude of operational agreements. Fortunately, your client has an impeccable record-keeping system.'

'I have been keeping a close eye on that process, thanks Lorenzo. I am impressed that you know exactly when and where you and your team need my or my client's input.'

*

The Sicilian mafia was well connected throughout Europe. They had several operatives in or near every single country. The United Kingdom was no exception.

Matteo Ricci took no time at all to establish that the unknown assailant who had shot Jason Jones was a short, overweight man with thinning red hair. The pilot. He reasoned that, since the pilot had been injured during his capture, he would be in a nearby prison hospital. There weren't many on that side of London, and by mid-afternoon the pilot's location had been pinpointed. Ricci despatched a local London mafia enforcer.

The mafia enforcer had no trouble with gaining access to the pilot's hospital room. His network of those on retainer from the mafia was extensive.

'Rome has sent me to question you.'

The pilot was instantly awake, his eyes wide and darting from side to side, looking for an escape. He went to rise and was immediately reminded that he was handcuffed to the hospital bed. His next instinct was to call out for help.

The mafia enforcer had anticipated this and placed one hand tightly over the pilot's mouth.

'No noise.' The Italian allowed the pilot to see the silencer gun in his shoulder holster.

The pilot nodded his head and the enforcer slowly removed his hand. He reached into his pocket and produced a roll of duct tape. In a well-practiced move, he secured a hastily drawn strip over the pilots' mouth.

'Just so we can talk without interruption. Capisce?'

The pilot remained motionless.

'Have you spoken to anyone from the authorities since you were brought in here late yesterday?'

The pilot shook his head.

'Stronzata, bullshit.' The enforcer punched the pilot in the stomach, resulting in a muffled bellow of pain. 'Shh. I am only just getting started. I know you had a visitor this morning.'

Tears were streaming down the pilot's severely bruised face as he nodded his head.

'Bene, good. Now I'm going to remove the tape so we can have a proper chat. I'll know if you're lying to me.'

The pilot nodded his head again as the duct tape was ripped off. He stifled a groan. 'I have had a visit from an Inspector Mason from UK INTERPOL.'

'Now we are getting somewhere. I heard you had a visit from a large Englishman with glasses and a thick grey moustache. Is that him?'

'Yes.'

'And what did you tell him?'

'Nothing, I swear.'

'I don't believe you.' The Italian raised his fist and readied another punch to David the pilot's midsection.

'I'm telling the truth.' David held up his hands in defence. 'I told him I would not tell him anything unless he had a written deal for me. It was just a delaying tactic until someone like you came and rescued me. I'm ready to go. Take me with you.'

'You have been most helpful, thanks.' The mafia enforcer replaced the duct tape over the pilot's mouth and reached into his coat pocket for a wrapped syringe. He carefully removed the wrapping and the cap on the syringe. With a vice-like grip he held the pilot's feet together with one hand and inserted the needle between his toes with the other.

The pilot's last thought as he experienced the symptoms of a massive heart attack was that this must have been what they did to Luna Smythe.

The mafia enforcer stayed long enough to ensure the success of his handywork and quietly left. He was able to exit by a rear entrance, unlocked by his contact. Once outside, he dialled Matteo Ricci's number. 'All done, boss.'

'Molto bene, very good. Arrivederci!.'

*

Inspector Mason returned to the prison hospital three hours after he had left. The pilot's bed was empty. He glared at the prison guard accompanying him. 'What the hell happened here? Where's my prisoner?' Mason was exhausted and wanted there to be no confusion about how he felt.

'I'm told he had a massive heart attack, guv. The prison doctor could not revive him, even with the defibrillator out in the hall. It all happened before my shift started.'

'Take me to the control room. I need immediate access to the camera feed.'

'Sure thing, guvnor. This way.'

Inspector Mason was not surprised to hear that there was a glitch with the recordings. For some unknown reason the entire camera network for the prison hospital wing had suffered a fifteen-minute outage.

He located the prison doctor and was told that the pilot had suffered a massive fatal heart attack. 'Commission an autopsy and an analysis of the contents of the pilot's intravenous drip. Look for puncture wounds anywhere on the body.'

The doctor looked up from the notes he was writing when Mason stopped talking.

'Got it?' Mason said more loudly than he had intended.

'Yes, sir.'

Inspector Mason left the prison, wondering if it had been the Sicilian mafia or the Colombian drug cartel who had killed the pilot. Mafia, most likely. *It matters not*, he thought. He's gone, along with all the valuable information he may have been able to impart.

Chapter 41

DAY 14 (Sunday)

Jackson had called the hospital late on Saturday and was told that Jones had slept most of the day. Hospital staff had just given him a heavy dose of pain killers together with a sedative to help him sleep. He was expected to sleep through the night. He decided to wait until the morning to visit his friend.

When Tom and Willow arrived at the hospital after breakfast they brought an extra cappuccino for Jones. Inspector Mason was already in the room.

'Morning, Jason, Inspector.' Jackson's smile faded when he saw the serious faces that greeted him. 'What's going on?'

'The inspector here has good news and bad. The bad news is that our short dumpy pilot friend has been sent to meet his maker. He apparently suffered a massive heart attack, and couldn't be revived.' Jason's eyes were expressionless.

'It looks like the same modus operandi as that used in the killing of Luna Smythe. Mafia most likely.' Mason was shaking his head.

'And the good news?' Jackson was still processing the significance of the pilot's death.

'Well, he did provide me with some very valuable information before telling me that further information would need to wait until I produced a written deal, which included witness protection.

He was convinced that without Jensen, Smythe or Xiao, Jensen's operation would end. That is, unless someone could promptly revive Jensen's secure network. He assured me that he was the only living person who had any prospect of doing so. Jensen apparently had absolute control over access protocols. Assuming he's right, and he would have no reason to lie about that, control of Jensen's secure network ended with the pilot's death and the destruction of Smythe's laptop. He was also certain that the Hong Kong-based syndicate ended with the deaths of Yen Chow Yu and Ping Xiaoyan. Again, he would have no reason to lie about that.'

'What makes you think he would know all this?' Tom wanted to be certain that what he was hearing was true.

'We can never be certain, of course.' Mason rubbed his chin aggressively, causing his large ears to move in unison. 'He was, however, the proverbial fly on the wall in many of Jensen's high-level conversations. Also Xiao's. In his own words, he said that one of the few advantages he had personally experienced of being short and overweight was that no one took him seriously. To many he was invisible. Highly confidential discussions took place as though he were not there. I was very keen to tap into his knowledge about the Colombian drug cartel and the Sicilian mafia. The deal I took to him was an attractive one.'

'Who would have thought he could be killed so easily in a prison hospital,' Willow said.

'Indeed. I went to look at the secure camera footage of the incident, and was told there had been a technical glitch and that fifteen minutes of footage for the hospital wing was missing. I will commission an investigation into the events.'

'While I'm pissed off about not getting any more information from the pilot, I'm not unhappy the little shit is gone. Lucky he's not a good shot!' Jones had more colour in his face as he sipped the coffee from Tom. 'Good news is we have reason to believe that Jensen's organisation and the Chinese syndicate may have finally both been dealt fatal blows.'

'I feel the same way, Jason.' Jackson was leaning back in his chair. 'As we have learnt from bitter personal experience, though, there are no guarantees. The mafia and drug cartels have been around for a long time, laundering their own ill-gotten gains. Let's hope we've seen the last of them for a while.'

'What do you want to do about security from here?' Willow crossed her arms.

Jones sat up a little. 'Good question, Willow. I spoke with the surgeon this morning, and he confirmed it should be safe for me to travel back to Aus around Friday this week. Maybe we can take the same flights from London to Sydney, Tom. Will that give you enough time to complete your transaction?'

'I think so, Jase. Even if we're not quite across the line by then, I should be able to effect completion remotely, with Lorenzo Bassutri's assistance. He's been extra helpful since he realised the significance of his disclosure of our whereabouts to his mafia family member. Jury's still out for me on whether he has anything other than a familial connection with the mafia. Regardless, I've been very careful to limit our interactions to professional matters only.'

'Very wise,' Inspector Mason chimed in.

'Okay then, Tom, let's make those travel arrangements, mate. Willow, until we leave on Friday, I suggest you keep a close eye on Tom at the safe house. Overkill, I'm sure, but let's keep Oliver's other two operatives active. One here at the hospital for my benefit, and the other with you and Tom at the safe house.'

'Roger that. I'll call it in to Oliver,' Willow responded on a high note. Tom sensed that her inner joy of spending a few more days together in the safe house matched his feelings.

'Agreed, Jason, and thanks, Willow. I'll smooth that over with the client. They are elated that the back-up deal has progressed so quickly. There has also been a favourable shift in the exchange rate of close to four per cent. That translates to around $12 million, which will more than make up for the reduction in price from the first to second deals.' Jackson was beginning to hope that the constant threat to his safety, and to those around him, may soon be over.

'I'll head back to base and get on with my further investigations and reporting. I'll also send an update to Inspector Darwin at Australian INTERPOL. He'll be delighted to hear all the latest news.'

'Thanks, Inspector. Let me know if you need anything further from Jason or me, and in particular before we head home at the end of the week. It's been a real pleasure working with you again. I'd be less than honest if I didn't say I hope that's close to the last time we need to discuss these matters.' Jackson shook hands with Inspector Mason.

'I hope so, too Tom. It does look like it, but we can never be certain.' Mason's jowls quivered as he laughed, although Tom noticed the inspector's eyes did not reflect his outward joviality.

Chapter 42

DAY 24 (Wednesday)

Ten Days Later

The remainder of the week in the London safe house was largely uneventful, at least in respect to any existential threats. Much of the work on Jackson's transaction had been done. He used the time to unwind and check on Jason Jones from time to time. Tom and Willow made the most of their voluntary confinement.

Jackson and his Italian colleague, Lorenzo Bassutri, were able to finalise the transaction for the sale of the Mondo Dei Sogni theme park near Rome. Completion took place on the Friday, not long before Tom and Jason Jones boarded the plane for the first leg of their international flight from London to Sydney.

Jones recovered well from his gunshot wound and promised Tom that he would continue his rest and recovery period after returning to Sydney. By Sunday evening, Jackson was safely in his own home in Brisbane.

On the Monday morning, Jackson had arrived at his office in central Brisbane early. He noticed that his colleague and good friend, Max Grenfell, was already in the office.

'Got a minute, Max?' Tom knocked on Max's open door.

'Tom. Holy shit, mate, it's good to see you.' Max Grenfell leapt out of his leather desk chair and covered the distance between him and Tom in two large strides. Before Jackson could step back, Max had embraced him in a man hug.

'Easy, Max.' Jackson laughed, freeing himself as he stepped back a little.

'Thanks for keeping me up to date with your whereabouts by email, Tom. I kept a close eye on the relevant news broadcasts. There's been a lot going down.'

'Spot on, Max. I couldn't divulge too much in my emails nor in the brief chat we had last week. Thanks for taking such good care of things here for me while I was away. It's always a bit of a risk to leave the office for any extended period of time. No telling what work or staff some of our fellow business proprietors might pilfer.'

'My pleasure, mate. Now sit down and tell me all the sordid details.' Max was chuckling at Tom's brutal assessment of some of their colleagues as he pointed to a lounge chair in the corner of his office.

'How much time have you got?'

Grenfell closed the door to his office and activated 'busy' mode on his work phone. 'As much as you need.'

Jackson spent the next hour and a half describing in detail the events that took place in Rome and London over the last two weeks. Grenfell sat spellbound with his mouth open for most of the time.

'Far out, Tom. That's another incredible story. Unbelievably dangerous. You might need to rethink how you approach these large deals of yours. I know being on site, and in the same time zone, is beneficial, but is it safe?'

'You're right, of course. No one could have predicted how things would have played out. Hopefully that really is the end of Murray Jensen's criminal organisation and the Hong Kong-based syndicate. I'll keep my head down for a little while, just in case.'

'And what about the Colombian drug cartel and the Sicilian mafia who between them lost €200 million?'

Jackson shrugged. 'Don't know for sure. We'll just have to see how that plays out over time.'

Grenfell shook his head in disbelief. 'Don't be too dismissive, Tom. They are two very powerful groups.'

'You don't need to tell me that, mate, after what I've been through over the last two weeks.' Jackson leaned back in the lounge. 'But on to more immediate matters. Hopefully you're planning to be at the partners' meeting on Wednesday. I plan to give an abridged version of the story I have just shared with you.'

'Wouldn't miss it for quids, mate.'

*

The managing partner of Ridgeway Mason's Brisbane office, Frederick Anderson, called the partners' meeting to order at five p.m. on the Wednesday. Around half the partners were in attendance. Another eight had indicated an intention to attend the meeting. One said that urgent work commitments may prevent her attendance. The remainder said they would be there, no doubt according to their own misguided interpretation of the meaning of punctuality.

Jackson met with Fred earlier in the day to let him know what he planned to report at the meeting that evening. He knew Fred didn't like surprises. Anderson told Tom that he wanted as many partners as possible to hear his report. He suggested that Tom's report be dealt with under general business, the last item on the agenda. That way, even the tardiest would have arrived by then.

The other items on the meeting agenda were dealt with in thirty minutes. By the time the general business section of the agenda was reached, all of those expected to arrive at the meeting had done so.

'Tom, from what you told me earlier today, you've had an interesting time. Care to share with your fellow partners?'

'Absolutely, thanks Fred.' Tom looked slowly around the twenty participants seated at the large timber boardroom table, locking eyes with each in turn. He knew at least four of his fellow partners loathed him and would like nothing more than to hear of a failed venture. Most had no idea of what might be included in Tom's report. He savoured the moment before delivering a precis of the events of the last couple of weeks. He could see that even his detractors were quietly in awe, unable to hide their true feelings.

'The client has agreed to pay my quoted fee of $1 million plus expenses, and an additional success fee of $4 million. Before you all rush to mentally bank the extra $4 million, I would like to again share it 75/25 with Jason Jones. Without him, I may not be here to give this report.'

Most of those around the table began to quietly applaud, even one of those who couldn't stand him. The other three sat stony-faced.

Frederick Anderson raised his hand for silence.

'You're making a habit of this, Jackson,' one of the stony-faced three sneered.

'I certainly hope so.' Anderson stood and shook Tom's hand. 'Unbelievable, Tom. Anyone not in favour of Tom's suggestion to share his success fee?' No one raised their hands.

As the meeting ended most of those present spoke with Tom and shook his hand, expressing a mixture of concern, awe and gratitude.

Jackson left the meeting without participating in the compulsory post meeting drinks. He wanted to call Jason Jones and tell him the good news.

'You're fucking kidding me, mate. One million fucking dollars. Are you sure?'

'Sure am, Jason. No need for you to share any of that with Oliver Planksmith this time. The client has separately paid them a bonus of twenty per cent. Rest up and enjoy. I plan to take a couple of weeks off soon. I'll head your way so that we can celebrate properly after you're up and about. I have something in mind I'd like to chat to you about.'

'Can't wait, mate. See you soon.'

As Jackson hung up the phone, he wondered how happy Jones would be when he actually heard what Tom needed to talk to him about. Or maybe he'd just park it until another day. He'd had more than enough on his plate of late, and wasn't entirely keen to add even more.

*

Pablo Barato, the head of security for the Colombian drug cartel, arrived at their remote operation deep in the Amazon jungle, east of Quito in Ecuador. Shortly after his meeting with representatives of the Sicilian mafia in Rome, he had directed that a thorough search be undertaken of the work area utilised by Luna Smythe while rebuilding Murray Jensen's secure network. Anything of remote interest was to be locked away until his arrival on site. He was accompanied by the cartel's tech expert.

The pair spent the next two days combing through everything Smythe had left behind. Initially it looked as if Smythe had successfully covered her electronic tracks, that is until the chance discovery of a small encrypted thumb drive taped to the underside of a cupboard in an adjoining kitchen area. Perhaps Luna Smythe had hidden the digital keys to the network as a contingency for her own protection. Once decrypted, the drive provided all of the necessary security protocols to access Jensen's entire network.

Barato couldn't wipe the sinister grin of his face as he stared at the thumb drive in the palm of his oversized hand.

Acknowledgements

Many thanks again to my very talented editor and independent publisher Dr Juliette Lachemeier from The Erudite Pen. I'm very grateful, Juliette, for your invaluable editorial input into bringing all three of my books to a successful reality. Your passion and attention to detail are extraordinary.

My thanks again to our good friend Julie Comans for the serendipitous introduction to Juliette.

Thank you, Judith San Nicolas from JudithSDesign&Creativity, for another impressive book cover.

Thanks also to all who have read my first two books, *Know Your Enemy* and *Beware Your Enemy*, and for your positive feedback. Particular thanks to my immediate family and close friends for your encouragement to continue my writing journey.

Last but not least, many thanks to those who've read this book. I hope you enjoyed it as much as I enjoyed writing it. It will help others to discover my books if you were able to kindly leave a star rating and/or review on Amazon or Goodreads.

A Tom Jackson Legal Thriller

ROD BESLEY

Know Your Enemy

Book 1 Available at all major booksellers

Book 2 Available at all major booksellers

ABOUT THE **AUTHOR**

Hailing from Australia, Rod Besley's unique background as an esteemed lawyer infuses his writing with a deep understanding of legal intricacies. His ability to unravel complex legal puzzles while keeping readers on the edge of their seats is a testament to his expertise and narrative finesse.

As the creative force behind *Know Your Enemy, Beware Your Enemy* and *Vanquish Your Enemy*, Rod invites readers to explore the high-stakes world of corporate transactions, espionage and unrelenting suspense. He has a knack for weaving intricate plots and delivering heart-pounding twists for legal-thriller enthusiasts. In the style of James Patterson, his novels deliver short, sharp chapters that are jam packed with action, intrigue and suspense.

Follow Rod's literary journey for a glimpse into the mind of a legal virtuoso turned storyteller. With each new release, he invites readers to dive headfirst into the realms of power, corruption and the relentless pursuit of truth. If you're a fan of gripping legal dramas that defy conventions, Rod's novels are a must-read for your bookshelf.

The author graduated with a combined law/accounting degree from the Australian National University. He has over thirty-five years of experience at prestigious law firms as a transaction lawyer. As a partner, he was regularly exposed to the 'cut and thrust' of huge transactions in one of the largest global law firms.

A skilled legal wordsmith and keen assessor of human behaviour, Rod now utilises this talent in fiction writing – developing characters and plots for legal thrillers.

Vanquish Your Enemy: A Tom Jackson Legal Thriller is Rod's third novel in the Tom Jackson series. Jackson is an esteemed transaction lawyer who becomes embroiled in an illegally funded 200 million Euro theme park sale. *Vanquish Your Enemy*, although entirely fictional, gives readers an insight into the high-stakes world of corporate transactions, espionage, intimidation and conspiracy.

Enjoyed the book? You can contact the author at:

Website: rodbesley.com

Email: rod.besley88@gmail.com

LinkedIn: Rod Besley

Facebook: Rod Besley Author:
https://www.facebook.com/profile.php?id=61550080172957

If you liked the book, please leave a review on Amazon, Goodreads or with the author directly. Reviews are invaluable in supporting an author's hard work and are greatly appreciated.

　　　　　　　　　　—